DEADLY ODDS

Cannon brushed back his jacket and settled his gunbelt comfortably on his hips. People stopped to watch in disbelief. They'd heard about gunfights in the streets of Dodge and Tombstone, but had never seen anything like it in St. Charles.

Clint stepped down into the street from the boardwalk, waiting for the foolish gambler to make the first move, and he did. He drew his gun with decent speed, but Clint drew his own gun and shot the man dead in his tracks before he could fire.

The crowd gasped as Clint walked to the fallen man and looked down at him. Before he could raise his head the onlookers began to scatter, as if afraid that the big bad gunman would turn his weapon on them.

Clint ejected the spent shell from his barrel and replaced it with a live one before holstering his gun.

"You should have stuck to cards," he told the dead man.

DON'T MISS THESE
ALL-ACTION WESTERN SERIES
FROM THE BERKLEY PUBLISHING GROUP

THE GUNSMITH by J. R. Roberts
Clint Adams was a legend among lawmen, outlaws, and ladies. They called him . . . the Gunsmith.

LONGARM by Tabor Evans
The popular long-running series about Deputy U.S. Marshal Long—his life, his loves, his fight for justice.

SLOCUM by Jake Logan
Today's longest-running action Western. John Slocum rides a deadly trail of hot blood and cold steel.

BUSHWHACKERS by B. J. Lanagan
An action-packed series by the creators of Longarm! The rousing adventures of the most brutal gang of cutthroats ever assembled—Quantrill's Raiders.

DIAMONDBACK by Guy Brewer
Dex Yancey is Diamondback, a Southern gentleman turned con man when his brother cheats him out of the family fortune. Ladies love him. Gamblers hate him. But nobody pulls one over on Dex . . .

WILDGUN by Jack Hanson
The blazing adventures of mountain man Will Barlow—from the creators of Longarm!

TEXAS TRACKER by Tom Calhoun
Meet J.T. Law: the most relentless—and dangerous—manhunter in all Texas. Where sheriffs and posses fail, he's the best man to bring in the most vicious outlaws—for a price.

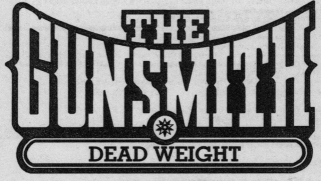

THE GUNSMITH

DEAD WEIGHT

J. R. ROBERTS

JOVE BOOKS, NEW YORK

THE BERKLEY PUBLISHING GROUP
Published by the Penguin Group
Penguin Group (USA) Inc.
375 Hudson Street, New York, New York 10014, USA
Penguin Group (Canada), 90 Eglinton Avenue East, Suite 700, Toronto, Ontario M4P 2Y3, Canada
(a division of Pearson Penguin Canada Inc.)
Penguin Books Ltd., 80 Strand, London WC2R 0RL, England
Penguin Group Ireland, 25 St. Stephen's Green, Dublin 2, Ireland (a division of Penguin Books Ltd.)
Penguin Group (Australia), 250 Camberwell Road, Camberwell, Victoria 3124, Australia
(a division of Pearson Australia Group Pty. Ltd.)
Penguin Books India Pvt. Ltd., 11 Community Centre, Panchsheel Park, New Delhi—110 017, India
Penguin Group (NZ), Cnr. Airborne and Rosedale Roads, Albany, Auckland 1310, New Zealand
(a division of Pearson New Zealand Ltd.)
Penguin Books (South Africa) (Pty.) Ltd., 24 Sturdee Avenue, Rosebank, Johannesburg 2196,
South Africa

Penguin Books Ltd., Registered Offices: 80 Strand, London WC2R 0RL, England

This is a work of fiction. Names, characters, places, and incidents either are the product of the author's imagination or are used fictitiously, and any resemblance to actual persons, living or dead, business establishments, events, or locales is entirely coincidental.

DEAD WEIGHT

A Jove Book / published by arrangement with the author

PRINTING HISTORY
Jove edition / November 2005

Copyright © 2005 by Robert J. Randisi.

ISBN: 0-515-14028-7

JOVE®
Jove Books are published by The Berkley Publishing Group,
a division of Penguin Group (USA) Inc.,
375 Hudson Street, New York, New York 10014.
JOVE is a registered trademark of Penguin Group (USA) Inc.
The "J" design is a trademark belonging to Penguin Group (USA) Inc.

PRINTED IN THE UNITED STATES OF AMERICA

10 9 8 7 6 5 4 3 2 1

PROLOGUE

Clint was seated in Rick's Saloon when the man came through the batwing doors.

The man was a stranger to him. He was in his early thirties, wearing a black suit with a white shirt. The first thing Clint noticed, however, was that the man was wearing an expensive rig on his hip, to accommodate what appeared to be an equally expensive gun. The handle of the pistol was mother-of-pearl, which Clint knew did not come cheap. It also wasn't smart to have such a surface on the handle of your gun. It was slippery, especially if your hand was sweating, but the man seemed to have countered that by wearing black leather gloves.

"Clint Adams?"

"That's right."

"They told me I'd find you out here," the man said. "My name is Martin Devlin, and I've come here to hire you. Are you available?'

"That would depend on the job." And how much he could get for it. Fact was he didn't really need any work at the moment. But he was always willing to listen.

"Have a seat," Clint invited. "Would you like a drink?"

"I could use a beer," Devlin said.

1

Clint waved to Colleen, one of the saloon girls, who came bustling over.

"Would you bring Mr. Devlin a beer, please?"

"Yes, sir," she said.

"Thank you."

As she walked away, Devlin watched her, then looked around the room for a moment.

"You got all these people cowed, don't you?"

"How do you mean?"

"Look at 'em," Devlin said, indicating the other men in the saloon. "They're all afraid of you."

"They've got nothing to be afraid of."

"That may be," Devlin said, "but they don't know that, do they?"

"That's their problem," Clint said. "Right now I thought we were here to talk about yours. You do have a problem, don't you?"

"Yeah, I do," Devlin said. He stopped as Colleen set his beer down in front of him. "Thanks."

She nodded and left them alone.

"I need you to come to St. Louis," Devlin said.

"What for?"

"Well . . . actually, it's not St. Louis, but just outside of St. Louis . . . I have a place, and somebody's trying to squeeze me out."

"Squeeze you out how?"

"Let's put it this way," Devlin said. "It's gonna come to gunplay."

"You strike me as the kind of man who can handle gunplay," Clint said.

"You're a good judge of character," Devlin said. "Yeah, I can handle myself with a gun, but I need more than just my own. I need men who can handle themselves—maybe even better than I can."

"Who else are you hiring?"

"I've got a few men in St. Loo already," Devlin said. "But I need someone to take charge of them."

"Are we talking about a range war?"

"Somethin' like that," Devlin said, "but you'd need to come and see for yourself."

"What are you paying?" Clint asked.

"My other men are getting a hundred a week."

"That's good money."

"I'll pay you a thousand."

"A week?"

"That's right."

Clint sat back. A thousand a week was hard to turn down.

"How many weeks?" he asked.

"As many as it takes."

"I'll need a guarantee."

"No problem," Devlin said. "I'll pay you five thousand, over and above a thousand a week. What do you say?" Devlin asked.

"It sounds like you have enough money to hire an army," Clint said. "Why not do that?"

"Because I don't want an army," Devlin said. "I want The Gunsmith, and I'm willin' to pay. So what do you say?"

Clint took a sip of beer, knew he should ask more questions, but said, "We can leave tomorrow."

Martin Devlin left Rick's and went directly to the telegraph office. He sent this telegram to St. Louis, Missouri: "HOOKED HIM, JUST HAVE TO REEL HIM IN." He signed it "Devlin."

He gave the flimsy to the clerk, who read it out loud to be sure he had it right, and then sent it.

"Will you be wantin' a reply?" the man asked.

"I don't expect one," Devlin said, "but if one does come in, leave it at my hotel."

"Yes, sir."

He left the telegraph office and walked over to the hotel.

Clint nuzzled Colleen's full breasts, rubbing his nose against her nipples as she giggled. He took each nipple into his mouth then, and sucked them until they were huge. She had the largest nipples he'd ever encountered, and they fascinated him.

Colleen was in her thirties, and her body was mature, which he liked. Full hips, a majestic butt and heavy breasts. He kissed his way down her body, until his face was nestled between her thighs. She reached down to hold his head while he licked her and sucked on her, until she squeezed his head between her thighs and cried out as her climax overcame her, wetting his mouth and face . . .

"What was that about, this afternoon?" she asked. "With that man."

"Just a job offer."

"Does that mean you're leavin' town?"

"For a while."

She sat up in bed and held her breasts in the palms of her hands, as if offering them to him.

"What could possibly take you away from these?" she asked, thumbing her nipples in a way she knew excited him.

"A thousand a week?"

She released her breasts and said, "That much? He must have a real problem on his hands."

Clint explained Devlin's problem to her.

"Sounds kind of vague," she said.

"For a thousand a week," Clint replied, reaching for her, "he can be vague."

"You're not hurting for money," she said, as he pulled her down on top of him.

Clint did have several bank accounts around the country and a good income from investments, but still . . .

"Maybe I'm just curious." He nuzzled her breasts again, once more toying with the objects of his fascination.

"Doesn't sound like your kind of job."

Clint bit her right nipple, causing her to gasp.

"Maybe I'm just bored."

"With me?" She slid her hand down between them to grasp his erect penis.

"Not with you," he said, "just with . . . things in general."

"Being bored," she whispered, sliding down between his legs, "could get you in a lot of trouble."

"What kind of trouble can I get in just being bored?" Clint asked his friend.

"I guess that remains to be seen," she said, just before engulfing him in her mouth.

ONE

"So you killed the man you were workin' for?" the sheriff asked.

Clint stared at the lawman, then turned his head to look out the window. The town of St. Charles, just outside of St. Louis, on the Missouri River, was going by. Men and women going on about their business, while he was in here answering questions.

"I told you," he explained. "Martin Devlin hired me to come here under false pretenses."

"What did he tell you he wanted you to do?" Sheriff Dan Jackson asked.

Jackson was in his thirties, a tall, broad-shouldered man who'd held his job for a couple of years. He'd braced Clint without fear, either because he didn't know who he was, or he didn't care. On his desk right now was Clint's gun and holster.

"He said he needed help," Clint said. "Somebody was trying to squeeze him."

"Squeeze him? In what way?"

"He didn't tell me," Clint said. "He said I'd have to see for myself."

"And you agreed on that basis?"

5

Clint felt foolish. He'd known at the time, in Labyrinth, that he should have asked more questions.

"I . . . He offered me a lot of money," Clint said.

"How much?"

"A thousand a week, above and beyond five thousand."

"How much did you get ahead of time?"

"A thousand."

"And when you got here?"

"There was no more money," Clint said.

"I don't understand how a man of your experience would get caught up in all this," Jackson said.

"Neither do I."

"All right, then," the lawman said, sitting back and crossing his arms, "explain it to me. What happened?"

Once they had arrived in St. Louis, Devlin had two horses waiting for them. They rode to St. Charles, where Devlin put Clint into a hotel and told him he'd see him in the morning.

Clint walked around the small river town of St. Charles that evening, had a meal, and then retired to his room for the night. He slept late the next morning, which he never did, and was feeling guilty when he came down to the lobby.

"Mr. Adams?" the clerk called out when he came down.

"Yes?"

"Someone to see you, sir."

Clint turned to look in the direction the clerk was pointing. He saw a man sitting on a divan in the lobby. He was dressed in the same manner Martin Devlin dressed—black suit, white shirt, string tie—but he wasn't Devlin. One other thing the two men had in common, however, was the gun on their hip.

The man stood as Clint approached him. His manner, the way he wore his gun, bespoke a man who was well acquainted with using one. Clint got a bad feeling.

"Are you looking for me?" he asked.

"I am if you're Clint Adams."

"I am."

"Then I need you out on the street."

"For what?"

The man grinned. He was Devlin's age, maybe a little younger, and he had the same arrogance.

"I'm gonna kill you."

Clint frowned and studied the man.

"Do I know you?"

"No," the man said, "we've never met. My name is Cannon, Dave Cannon."

"Should I know you?"

"Oh no," Cannon said, "no reason why you should have heard of me at all, Mr. Adams. But I've heard of you."

"So what's the reason you want to kill me?"

"What's the reason for anything?" the man asked. "Money. It's the only reason I do anything."

"I don't understand."

"You don't have to."

"Yes, I do," Clint said. "You see, if you make me step out into the street with you, I'm going to end up killing you, and before I kill a man I like to know why I'm doing it."

"I guess that makes sense," Cannon said. "Devlin didn't tell you why?"

"Devlin?" Clint asked, frowning. "What's Martin Devlin have to do with this?"

"Everything," the man said. "See, the first part of the bet was that he'd get you here. I lost that one. The second part of the bet, though . . . that one I intend to win."

"This is . . . a bet?"

"Life's a bet, Adams," Cannon said. "Yeah, Devlin bet me twenty thousand dollars that he could get you here. Now we're goin' double or nothin' that I can kill you in a fair fight."

Clint was starting to get it, and he was starting to feel foolish, as well as angry.

"You and Devlin, you're gamblers?"

"Now you've got it."

"And you're both so bored with cards and dice and other forms of gambling that you came up with this scheme?"

"You're a legend of the Old West, Adams," Cannon said. "You've killed more men than we can count. If one of us kills you, well . . ."

"And if I kill you?"

Cannon spread his hands and smiled.

"That's the gamble," he said. "What's a bigger thrill then gambling with your life?"

"Look," Clint said, "I don't mind if you and Devlin want to gamble with your own lives, but not mine."

"Too late," Cannon said. "See, you can't leave this hotel without something happenin'. Once you come out the door, I'm drawin' on you. The only way for you to come out of this alive is if you outdraw me."

"And if I kill you? Devlin wins the money?"

"No," Cannon said. "The money's bein' held by an intermediary. If you kill me, Devlin has to kill you to get it."

"And if I kill you both?"

"That's unlikely," Cannon said, "but we've made plans for that, too."

Clint stared at the man for a few seconds. His face was expressionless, but he was feeling anger and disbelief.

"You two," Clint said, "you're years late and miles away from the Wild West."

"That's why we brought it to us," Cannon said, "in you."

Clint shook his head.

"I'll be waitin' for you outside, Adams," Cannon said. "And let me say, it's been a real pleasure meetin' you."

The man turned and walked out of the hotel, Clint just staring after him. He'd been totally conned, and all because of the money. Now he was going to have to kill these two men, simply to restore his own self-respect, and he hated them for putting him in this situation.

He was indeed mad enough to kill . . .

TWO

"So you killed him?"

"He was standing out in the street, waiting, preening," Clint said, "posing . . ."

"And you were angry."

"Yes."

"Angry enough to kill?"

"Oh, yes."

"What happened?"

"It was quick . . ."

Cannon brushed back his jacket and settled his gunbelt comfortably on his hips. People stopped to watch in disbelief. They'd heard about gunfights in the streets of Dodge and Tombstone, but had never seen anything like it in St. Charles.

Clint stepped down into the street from the boardwalk, waiting for the foolish gambler to make the first move, and he did. He drew his gun with decent hand speed, but Clint drew his own gun and shot the man dead in his tracks before he could fire.

The crowd gasped as Clint walked to the fallen man and looked down at him. Before he could raise his head, the onlookers began to scatter, as if afraid that the big bad gunman would turn his weapon on them.

Clint ejected the spent shell from the barrel and replaced it with a live one before holstering his gun.

"You should have stuck to cards," he told the dead man, and then went in search of Martin Devlin.

It wasn't yet noon, but he found the gambler in a saloon several blocks from the hotel. He'd left Cannon in the street for others to take care of, and was mindful of wanting to find Devlin before the law found him.

The man was sitting at a table with four other men, playing poker. When Clint walked in, he folded his hand and sat back in his chair.

"I knew you'd take him."

"You owe me money."

"I gave you a thousand dollars."

"You still owe me five," Clint said. "You won your bet. Pay me and I'll be on my way."

"Oh, I didn't win my bet yet," Devlin said. "There's one more thing I have to do."

"That's not going to happen, Devlin."

"You're not gonna fight me?"

"You've got two choices, and two choices only," Clint said. "You can pay me and I'll be on my way, or you can die."

Devlin smiled. The other men at the table began to collect their money and steal away. Others in the saloon either left or sought refuge against the wall, out of the line of fire.

"Well," Devlin said, "I'm not payin' you, that's for sure."

"That leaves you with one choice."

"Let's do it, then," Devlin said, standing up. "I'll meet you on the street."

"You first."

Devlin stared at him.

"You think I hedged my bet?" he asked. "Maybe I've got a man on the roof with a rifle?"

"Could be."

"I'm a gambler, Clint," Devlin said. "It's how I make my livin'—and I don't cheat. I'm not a cheap tinhorn."

"That remains to he seen."

"Like I said, I'll see you on the street."

He walked past Clint and out the saloon door . . .

"So you killed him, too."

"He and Cannon were basically the same person."

"I could have told you that," Jackson said, "if you had asked me."

"He was out there, looked like he was waiting for someone to take his photograph. They both thought all it took to kill a man was to get their gun out first."

"Devlin was pretty good," Jackson said. "I've seen him shoot."

"Not good enough, I'm afraid," Clint said. "Oh, he was fast—faster than Cannon. But he wasn't fast enough."

"By the time I reached Cannon's body, you were gone," Jackson said. "Some folks who saw what happened told me about it, and pointed the way you'd gone. I heard the shots from the saloon, came running and found you standing over Martin Devlin."

Jackson had asked Clint for his gun, which he'd handed over. They'd walked to the sheriff's office together while some men collected the bodies from the street.

"This is St. Charles, Mr. Adams," Sheriff Jackson said, "not Wichita, not Dodge City, and not Tombstone."

"You forgot Leadville."

"My point is, I can't have bodies in the streets."

"Won't be anymore, as far as I'm concerned," Clint said. "In fact, these two weren't my idea."

"No," Jackson said, "from what I can determine, you're right—but I still have to ask you to leave St. Charles."

"I wouldn't have it any other way, Sheriff," Clint said. "There's nothing keeping me here, and I'm not going to have very fond memories of the place."

"Can't say I blame you for that."

Clint stood.

"I will be needing my gun, though."

Now Jackson stood, and the two men faced each other over his desk, where the gun and holster still lay. Finally, Jackson picked it up and held it out to Clint, who accepted it.

"When will you be leaving?" he asked.

"As soon as I leave your office, I'm checking out of the hotel and heading back to St. Louis to catch the next train west." He strapped on his gunbelt.

"That suits me."

Clint turned and headed for the door. The two men knew there was no need for a handshake, or another word. They'd never see each other again, and that was just fine with them both.

THREE

Clint got to St. Louis before dark, secured a hotel room for himself and went out in search of a meal. St. Louis was too close to the Mississippi for his liking, too much like a modern city of the East. He was anxious to return to the West. Kansas and Oklahoma were not so far from Missouri, but they managed to be different—different enough, anyway—but he was yearning for Arizona, Texas and New Mexico. All he had to show for this foolish trip to Missouri was a thousand dollars and two dead men. All he wanted from this place now was a meal and a good night's sleep, and then he'd be on his way.

He decided not to eat in any of the big restaurants he passed. Instead, he figured to find himself a small café down by the river, where maybe folks wouldn't find him so attention-worthy . . .

Rachel Chandler sat on the box, looking around at the activity going on. She'd asked a couple of men for help early on, but they'd turned her down. As beautiful as she was, they just didn't want to get involved, especially considering the box she was seated on.

Now she'd been sitting there for hours, flies buzzing around her, clothes sticking to her damp skin, not knowing what she was going to do. There was no way she could get off this riverfront on her own, that was for sure.

13

Apparently, she hadn't thought this through all that well . . .

Clint came out of the Second Street Café, satisfied with the bowl of beef stew he'd found inside. That bowl of stew would probably be the only good memory he'd have of Missouri.

He decided to take a walk down by the docks, and that's when he saw the woman sitting right in the center of all the dockside activity. Men were walking around her, avoiding her with such practiced ease that he had the feeling they'd been doing it most of the day.

She appeared to be a very pretty woman in her late twenties or early thirties. Her long dark hair was hanging limp and damp from the heat, and her dress was stained with patches of perspiration. The dress molded itself to her body, so that men cast admiring glances her way, even as they were stepping around her. But still, no one was stopping to speak to her, to offer her help in any way. You'd think in a bunch of men there'd be one who'd want to help a pretty lady, but that fact that they didn't probably had more to do with the plain pine coffin she was sitting on than anything else.

"Ma'am."

She looked up at him, his shadow shielding her from what was left of the sun.

"You look like you could use some help."

"Well," she said, "there's an astute observation. I've been sitting here for hours, ever since the riverboat left me here this morning."

"Do you mind if I ask you what, or who, is in the coffin, ma'am?" Clint asked.

"If you'll stop callin' me ma'am," she said. "My name is Rachel Chandler—Mrs. Chandler. It's my husband who's in the coffin."

"Oh," Clint said.

She stared at him.

"You're not gonna apologize?"

"For what?" he asked. "I didn't kill him."

"Good point," she said, "but you are the only man today

who has spent more than three minutes talking to me . . . and not leering at me."

"That was just my curiosity."

"And has it been satisfied?" she asked.

Clint looked around. It was as if he had been absorbed into the woman's world. Not only were men walking around her, they were walking around him, too.

"If I turn and walk away, what are you going to do?" he asked.

"Just sit here, I guess," she said. "I can't very well move Ethan myself."

"Ethan?"

She knocked on the lid of the coffin and said, "My husband."

"Oh," he said, "well, no, I guess you couldn't."

"I bet you could, though."

"Move it, you mean?"

"Uh-huh."

"Well, I suppose I could. Where would you like it moved to? Just off the dock?"

"No," she said, "how about . . . Texas?"

Clint hesitated, not sure he'd heard right, then said, "Oh, sorry?"

"My husband was from Texas," she said. "That's where he wanted to be buried, and I promised to take him there." She stomped one foot on the dock. "This is as far as I've gotten, so far."

"How were you planning on going?"

"The train, naturally," she said. "How else?"

"So . . . you just have to get this thing to the railroad station?" Clint asked.

"I suppose that would be the first step," she said. "Then I'd have to find out when the next train leaves that's going west."

"Well," Clint said, "I guess I could help you get the coffin to the station."

"Why would you do that?" she asked. "I mean, I could pay you something . . . a little . . . for your help, but . . ."

Clint also wondered why he was offering to help this woman rather than walking around her like all the other men were. Maybe it was because he'd just killed two men and was angry about it. Not so much angry that he'd killed them—he'd killed men before, in defense of his life—but because of the way he had been brought to the situation.

Or, on the other hand, maybe he just didn't want to be like all these other men.

"So?" she asked, and he became aware that it was the second time she'd said it.

"So what?"

"Are you offering me your help?"

"Yes," he said, without hesitation. "Yes, I am."

"Then I accept." She stood up and put her hand out to him. "I told you my name is Rachel Chandler. My husband's name was Ethan."

"Clint," he said, shaking her hand, "Clint Adams, and I suppose the first thing we need to do is get ahold of a buckboard."

FOUR

Dutch Crater looked down at his youngest son, lying on his back amid filthy, sweat-stained sheets. The nineteen-year-old was covered with slippery perspiration, and his face was a rosy color from the fever that was raging within him.

"Dutch."

He ignored the voice at first, until it called his name again.

"Dutch!"

He turned and looked at Doc Tappin, standing directly behind him, towering over him from his height of six-foot-eight.

"There's nothin' you can do for the boy," the doctor said. "Go home and get some sleep."

Dutch turned and looked down at the boy again.

"Can you guarantee me that he'll be alive when I come back?" he asked.

The doctor hesitated, then said, "Well, no, I can't. Fact is, I don't know if the boy is gonna pull through. That bullet is still in there, and if I try to take it out while he's in this condition, I'll probably kill him."

"Then I'll stay."

"He doesn't know you're here, Dutch," Tappin said. "His fever's so high—"

"Are my boys outside?" Dutch asked.

"One of them is."

At that Dutch turned and glared at the doctor.

17

"One?"

Tappin nodded and said, "Luke."

Luke was the oldest.

"Where are the other two?"

Tappin shrugged. "I guess they . . . they probably went to get somethin' to eat—"

"Went to get drunk, is more likely." Dutch Crater stood up. He was almost as foot shorter than the doctor, but he outweighed him by quite a bit. "Stay with him. I'll be right back."

"Sure . . ."

Dutch went by the doctor and out into the next room. He found his oldest boy, Luke, waiting there with Del Crockett. Del wasn't one of his sons, but he might as well have been. He and Luke had been best friends since they were kids.

"Where are your brothers?" Dutch demanded of Luke.

"I tried to tell them to stay, Pa," Luke said, "but they wanted to go and, uh, get somethin' to eat—"

"They're more than likely at Rosie's, whorin' and drinkin'," Dutch said. "That's where they want to be if and when their brother draws his last breath?"

"Aw, Pa, Billy ain't gonna die—"

"I got news for you, Luke," Dutch said. "It's likely he is gonna die, and I want all of ya here if he does. You go and get your brothers and bring 'em here."

"What if they don't wanna come, Pa?"

Dutch looked at Del, then back at Luke.

"You and Del do what you gotta do to make 'em come, you hear?" he said. "I want 'em here!"

"Yes, Pa," Luke said. He looked at Del, jerked his head and the two men left. Dutch turned and went back into the room where his youngest son lay dying.

When he entered, Doc Tappin moved away from the bed to make room for him.

"What are you gonna do, Dutch?" he asked.

"I'm gonna sit here until the boy dies, or wakes up," Dutch said.

"Then what?"

Dutch looked up at the man over his shoulder.

"Then I'm gonna track down the person responsible for

this," he said. "There's a debt owed here, and I'm gonna make sure that debt gets paid.

Luke and Del found the other two boys, Coy and Sam, right where their father said they'd be, at Rosie's, with a whore in one hand and a drink in the other. They were sitting in the parlor, but Luke knew they were only a few minutes from heading for the second floor.

"Time to go, boys," he said.

Luke and Del were the same age, twenty-six. Coy was twenty-three, Sam two years younger. Of the four Crater boys, Luke was the only one who favored his father, shorter than the others, but wider, with a broad chest and tree-trunk thighs.

"We ain't gone upstairs yet, Luke," Coy said.

"And you ain't gonna," Luke said. "Pa wants both of you over to the doc's."

"What for?" Sam asked. "Is Billy awake?"

"He ain't awake, and he ain't liable to be," Luke said. "Billy's probably gonna die."

"Then what do we have to be there for?" Coy asked. "Come on, Luke, you and Del grab yourselves a gal and—"

Luke stepped forward and cut his brother off by grabbing the front of his shirt and hauling him to his feet. The girl sitting with him yelled and went flying off the sofa. Her dress was so low-cut that her chubby breasts popped free. Behind Luke, Rosie stood, her chins quivering. She was tempted to call for her security man, but she knew he'd probably get stomped by Luke Crater and Del Crockett. Better to let the scene play itself out.

"Pa said we should get you to the doc's any way we can, Coy," Luke said. "You know what that means?"

"Hey, Luke" Sam said, "take it easy—"

But he was cut off in much the same way his brother Coy had been, when Del stepped forward and hauled him to his feet. Sam was the shortest of the men and his feet were almost dangling.

"Okay, okay," Coy shouted. "Jeez, we'll come with ya, if Pa said we wuz ta."

"He did."

Luke released his brother and shoved him toward the door. Sam soon followed.

Outside, as they walked from the whorehouse to the doctor's office, Coy asked, "When we goin' after 'em, Luke?"

"When Pa says."

"We gotta go downriver, ya know," Coy said, "to St. Louis. We wait too long and we're gonna lose—"

"We ain't gonna do nothin' until Pa tell us to, Coy," Luke said. "You got that?"

"Sure, I got that, Luke," Coy said. "That's how we live most of our lives."

Luke turned on his brother. "And, boy, that's how you're gonna live the rest of your life, too. Now shut the hell up."

"Hey, Luke—" Sam started.

"Both of you!" Luke screamed.

Silently, they continued their walk to the doctor's office.

FIVE

It was almost dusk by the time Clint was able to return to the docks with a buckboard. He'd had to walk several blocks before he came to a livery, and then that one didn't have a buckboard for rent. He obtained directions, though, to a place that did, and then had to return to the livery to rent a horse.

"I was starting to think you weren't coming back," Rachel said when he returned.

He explained what he'd gone through to obtain both buckboard and horse.

"I'll have to give you the money for them," Rachel said.

"Let's get your husband up onto the buckboard and off the dock before we talk about that."

"You'll need help—" she started, but stopped when Clint bent at the knees, grasped the handle of the coffin, tested it to make sure it would hold, and then hoisted the coffin up off the ground, almost up onto one shoulder. He only had to walk a short distance with it, or he might have looked around for help. Rachel was surprised that Clint had been able to lift it. He certainly seemed big enough, but she'd still expected him to need at least one other man.

For his part Clint wondered how big a man Ethan Chandler had been. The coffin was heavy, but not as heavy as he'd expected. He'd only meant to test the weight of it before getting help, but as it turned out, he'd been able to handle it. Maybe the man had wasted away, lost most of his weight before he died.

He turned to find Rachel staring at him.

"Next stop, the railroad station," he said. "Can I help you up?"

"This is terrible!" Rachel said.

"It's not so bad," Clint said. "Next train leaves in the morning."

"I wanted to get started today."

"This way," Clint said, "you can get a good night's sleep and start out fresh. You've been sitting on that dock all day, and you probably want a bath."

"Oh," she said, rolling her eyes, "a bath would be heaven, but . . . what do we do with my husband?"

"I'm sure we can leave the buckboard behind the hotel overnight," Clint said.

"And what about you?" she asked. "Will you be leaving tonight?"

"I'll be leaving tomorrow, as well."

"On the same train?"

"Very likely."

"Then you'll be able to help me in the morning?"

"We'll be going to the same place," he said. "I don't see why not."

"I'll pay you—"

"Let's talk about it later, Mrs. Chandler—"

"Rachel," she said. "You must call me Rachel."

"Rachel, then," he said. "Do you have a preference for a hotel?"

"I don't know St. Louis very well," she said. "I came downriver from Alton."

"Well," Clint said, "I'm sure the ticket clerk can recommend a place. Why don't you wait here and I'll go back inside and ask?"

"All right," she said. "Thank you . . . Clint."

Clint went back inside to talk to the clerk.

"Back so soon?" the man in the blue cap asked. "Still no train tonight."

"I'll need two tickets for the morning train," Clint said, "and your recommendation for a hotel."

They completed their transaction for the tickets, and then the clerk said, "The Dock House is the closest, if you ain't particular."

"Is it cheap?" Clint didn't know how much money Rachel Chandler had. She already owed him for the horse, buckboard and ticket.

"Cheap as they come."

"Much obliged."

He returned to the buckboard and climbed up onto the seat next to Rachel.

"Here's your ticket," he said, handing one to her.

"And a hotel?"

"There's one nearby," Clint said.

He shook the reins at the horse and, as they started forward, felt Rachel lean her weight against him. It was warm, and not unpleasant.

"I can't stay here," Rachel said, looking at the place Clint had pulled to a stop in front of.

It was a falling down wreck of a hotel, probably meant more for dockworkers than anyone else. The saloon next door was rowdy with activity, and drunken men were already whistling and hooting at Rachel from the door.

"No, I don't suppose you can. My hotel is further, if you don't mind the ride . . . and it might be a bit more expensive."

"I'd like very much to stay at the same hotel as you, Clint," Rachel said.

"All right, then," Clint said. "That's where we'll go, then."

He wondered how the people at his hotel would like having a coffin out back overnight.

SIX

The clerk at Clint's hotel balked at having the coffin out back.

"I don't know if my boss would like it," the man said.

"Is your boss here tonight?"

"Well, no—"

"When will he be back?"

"Tomorrow, but—"

"Then he won't know anything about it, will he?"

"But, the guests, one of them might—"

"The guests are only going to see it if they happen to look out their back window," Clint said, "and I'll put the buckboard in the shadows. Don't worry."

He slipped a few bills across the desk to the man before he could protest further, and when the man saw them, he snatched them up and didn't say another word.

Clint took the key to Rachel's room off the counter and returned to where she was seated in the lobby.

"Here's your key. Do you need help going upstairs?"

"I only have a small bag."

Indeed, Clint had marveled at how light Rachel Chandler was traveling, unlike most women he'd known.

"I'll take the buckboard around to the back and then go directly to my room. I'm in room fourteen if you need anything."

She looked at the key in her hand, which had the number "19" attached to it.

25

"All right," she said. "Thank you."

"You can arrange with the clerk for a bath."

"May I buy you dinner after?" she asked.

"That's not necessary—"

"I have to settle up with you for the money you've expended so far," she said.

"And I am rather hungry . . . aren't you?"

He realized at that moment that he was extremely hungry.

"All right," he said. "Come to my room after your bath, and we'll come down to the dining room together."

"That's wonderful," she said. "I'll see you in a little while."

Clint walked to the front door, then turned to see her talking to the clerk. When she turned and saw him watching her, she waved and then carried her small carpetbag up the stairs.

Clint went outside and drove the buckboard around to the back of the hotel.

The dockworkers noticed the man immediately. In fact, he reminded them of the other man they'd seen earlier, the one who had helped the woman. Both had the same look in their eyes, like they'd take no shot from anybody. Both were tall, well built, but this one was dressed all in black while the other had worn a blue shirt and red bandanna, and this one was almost twenty years younger.

The other difference was that the older man had not approached any of them, and this one walked right up to them.

"I'm lookin' for someone," he said.

"That so?" There were four of them, and they closed ranks as one of them spoke. They were burly men who worked loading and unloading cargo from the riverboats, but none of them was wearing a gun, and the man in black was.

"A woman, long black hair, very pretty."

None of them answered.

"She has a coffin with her," the man went on. "Someone here must have taken it off the boat for her."

"Oh, yeah," the spokesman said, "her."

"Then you've seen her?"

"Like you said," another spoke up. "We took the coffin off the boat for her."

"And then what?"

"And then she sat on it on the dock all day."

"Why was that?"

"She wanted help gettin' it to the rail station," a third man said, "but we ain't supposed to leave the docks."

The man looked around, didn't see the woman or the coffin on the docks.

"So how did she get it moved?"

"A man came along and helped her."

"A man," the fourth one said, "like you. Wearin' a gun."

"He moved it himself?"

"Got a buckboard, hoisted it up on his shoulder and loaded it."

"We appreciate a fella knows how to lift."

"Any of you know this man?"

"No," the first man said. "Never saw him before."

"Do you know where they went?"

"They just . . . left."

"Probably went to the railroad station," one of them offered.

The man frowned. "Yes, they probably did."

With that he turned without so much as a thank-you and walked off the docks. The four men wished they could be there when the two gunmen met and fought over the woman.

They wondered if this one was the boyfriend, since the husband had been in the coffin.

It was a half an hour before there was a knock on Clint's door. He'd never known a woman to be able to take a bath that short. Rachel Chandler was turning out to be different in many ways.

"Finished already?" he asked.

"Yes," she said, "it was wonderful." She was wearing a clean, violet-colored dress and her hair smelled freshly washed—or maybe the smell was just coming from all of her.

"Let me get my hat and gun," he said, without inviting her into his room.

She waited in the hall until he joined her, and Clint closed his door behind them.

"Do you always wear your gun?" she asked. "Even in a city like St. Louis?"

"Yes," he said. "Always."

She hesitated a moment, torn by the desire to ask him why, then decided against it . . . for now.

"Shall we go and eat?" she asked.

"After you . . ."

SEVEN

At dinner Rachel gave in to the urge and finally asked Clint what he did for a living.

"This and that," he said.

She waited, and when he was not forthcoming with anything, she prompted, "And?"

"And not much else. Why do you want to know?"

"I'm curious," she said. "You helped me, today, you're still helping me. I feel I should know something about you. Don't you want to know about me?"

"Yes," he said. "Tell me about you."

She sat back and blinked, for a moment.

"All right," she persisted, "but answer a question for me."

"Very well," he said. "One."

"What did you do for a living before you did . . . this and that?"

"I've done many things," he said, "most of them having to do with a gun."

"Then you're . . . a gunman?"

"Not exactly."

"But—"

"That was a second question," he said.

"You still haven't really answered the first."

He took a deep breath, sat back in his chair and remained silent.

"All right, then," she said, "what do you want to know?"

By the time they got to dessert, he knew she'd been an only child, married young to get away from her abusive father, but married an older man, so that their marriage only lasted ten years before he died.

"The last thing he said to me was that he wanted to be buried in Texas, where he was born," she said, "so I felt it was the least I could do since he probably saved my life by marrying me."

"And your father?" Clint asked. "Is he still alive?"

"No," she said, "the dirty old bastard died a year before my husband did. That was probably the happiest day of my life."

They finished their pie, paid the bill and walked out into the lobby.

"This is going to sound silly," she said, 'but I'd like to check on Ethan, and say good night. Is there a back door?"

"Let's ask the clerk."

There was, indeed, a back door, and a few more dollars in the clerk's pocket gave them unlimited access to it. Clint led the way down the hall and out into the back, where the buckboard was tucked away in a corner, close to the base of the hotel so that it could not be seen from any of the windows. He'd unhitched the horse, and reminded himself now to slip yet a few more dollars to the clerk to have someone come and feed the animal.

Rachel walked to the coffin and put her hand on the smooth wood of the lid. It was a plain pine box, but the surface seemed to have been lovingly sanded to a smooth finish.

"Good night, sweetheart," she said to the box. "Tomorrow we begin our journey to Texas."

She patted the top of the coffin, then turned to face Clint. She looked very lovely with just a sliver of moonlight illuminating the pale skin of her face.

"I can't tell you how much I appreciate all your help," she said. "I'm afraid I was rather harsh with you when we first met."

"You'd had a rough day," he said.

"Yes," she said, "I did, but it has ended quite nicely, thanks to you." She approached him and kissed his cheek. "Thank you."

They went back into the hotel and he walked her back to her room. By the time he'd gotten into his own room, and into his bed, he remembered that they had not settled her financial debt to him.

EIGHT

Frank Magellan—the man in black—stopped at the railroad station even though there was no longer a clerk on duty. Before leaving, the clerk had pulled a shutter down over his window, and on the wood was the schedule of trains stopping in St. Louis the next day, along with their ultimate destinations. Magellan stopped to read the schedule, and was disappointed that only the final destination was listed and not stops along the way. He finally decided that he was going to have to return to the station the next morning, before the first train arrived. It looked like the only way to find out what train Rachel Chandler would be taking, with her coffin.

After leaving the station, he walked a few blocks, until he came to a run-down hotel. The only thing to recommend the place was that it was the closest hotel to the station, and that suited him just fine. He went inside, got himself a room and then immediately went to it to turn in for the night. Normally, he would have gone out looking for a saloon, or a girl or both, but he had to be up very early the next morning to be at the station before the first train.

This was business, and fun would save to wait.

Doc Tappin leaned over Billy Crater, pressed his head to the boy's chest, then reached for a mirror and held it beneath the patient's nose. Finally, he straightened, setting the mirror down, and turned to face Dutch Crater, hoping the man wouldn't kill him.

"I did everythin' I could, Dutch," he said. "The boy's dead."

Dutch pushed past Tappin, stood looking down at his dead son's face, then turned and went out into the outer room. Tappin breathed a sigh of relief, and closed the door behind Dutch, hoping the man would not come back in.

He turned to prepare Billy for his trip to the undertaker's.

"Pa?" Luke said, as Dutch came out.

"Your brother's dead," Dutch Crater said.

"Finally," Coy said, getting up from the chair he'd been sitting in and stretching. "Can we leave now?"

Dutch took one step and punched Coy in the face, knocking the boy over the chair and onto the floor. Blood from his nose smeared his mouth and chin.

Dutch turned and looked at Sam.

"You got anything to say?"

"I-I'm sorry, Pa," Sam said.

Dutch glared at him, then said, "Help your brother up." He turned to look at Luke.

"What do we do now, Pa?"

"We're gonna bury your brother tomorrow, and then go downriver to St. Louis."

"You think she's gonna be there?" Del asked.

"No," Dutch said, "but that's where we'll pick up her trail."

"And what are we gonna do when we catch her?" Luke asked.

"I don't know," Dutch Crater said, "but I'll figure it out by the time we do."

Dutch had the boys carry Billy's body over to the undertaker's and tell the man that the body had to be buried in the morning, at first light. Once they left, he turned to the doctor.

"Time to settle up, Doc," he said.

"That's okay, Dutch," Tappin said. "You don't owe me anything. I was glad to try to help."

"That's just it, Doc," Dutch said. "You tried, but you didn't help much, did you?"

"Uh, Dutch—"

"You're a doctor, you were supposed to keep him from dying," Dutch said, "and you didn't. For that I owe you."

"Dutch, don't—"

Dutch drew his gun and blew a hole in the doctor's chest.

"Heal yerself," he said, and walked out.

At the sound of the shot, Sam turned his head to look back at the doctor's office, and almost dropped his brother.

"Sam!" Luke said. "Pay attention."

"Did Pa . . . did he just kill the doc?" Sam asked.

"Some doctor," Luke said. "He let Billy die, he got what he deserved."

"What about Rachel, Luke?" Sam asked.

"What about her?" Coy said. "Damn, this boy wasn't this heavy when he was alive."

"What's Pa gonna do to her?"

"I guess it's like Pa said," Luke replied. "We'll find out when we do catch up to her."

NINE

Clint woke the next morning as first light streamed through his window. He was looking forward to getting back to Labyrinth, but was upset that he had come all this way and only had a thousand dollars—less his expenses—to show for it. A thousand dollars was not enough to make up for having to kill two men. He'd made a mistake taking this job, a bad one.

And while he was thinking about money, he had to remember to collect what Rachel owed him for the money he'd laid out the day before. She was pretty enough, and she was certainly a damsel in distress, but he wasn't about to go out-of-pocket for her—not to the tune of a buckboard, a horse and a hotel room.

He washed up, got dressed, collected his gear and left his room to go down the hall and see if she was awake, and ready to leave . . .

Once she was sure Clint had gone to his room the night before, Rachel had sneaked back downstairs and along that hallway to the back door. She was nervous about leaving the coffin outside unattended, so she brought the blanket from her hotel room with her, climbed into the back of the buckboard and bedded down next to the box.

"I'm not about to let anything happen to you," she said, soothingly, rubbing her hand along the pine.

Before going to sleep, she reached beneath her skirt and touched the two-shot derringer she had secreted there in a garter . . .

In the morning she woke before first light, feeling oddly refreshed from sleeping outside. She sneaked back into the hotel and up to her room, pausing only at Clint's door to press her ear to it. She heard nothing, so assumed he was not a noisy sleeper. She continued down the hall to her own room, then used the pitcher and basin on the dresser to freshen up. By the time she was done, she was sure she did not look like someone who had slept in a buckboard all night.

She settled down to wait for his knock at her door. She was famished, and knew they had enough time to get some breakfast before heading for the train station.

Magellan woke the next morning with plenty of time to get some breakfast before he had to be at the train station. He'd slept in his underwear because he didn't have any extra clothes with him. He really had not expected this job to take him out of town, and it still might not if he could stop the girl at the train. The only problem might be the man who was with her, but he wouldn't be able to judge that without seeing the man first.

He decided to make a hot breakfast his first priority, and then head for the train station.

Dutch Crater woke with a pounding headache, a result of all the whiskey he'd consumed the night before. But the whiskey hadn't helped. He'd still dreamed about his ex-wife, who had berated him mercilessly for letting their youngest boy—"her baby"—get killed. What right did that bitch have to complain; she had up and died of a fever years ago, leaving them all to fend for themselves.

Dutch staggered out of the shack he lived in with the boys, went to the nearest horse trough and dunked his head into it. When he came up for air, he slicked his hair back and looked up at the sky. He wanted to catch the first riverboat downriver from Alton to St. Louis, so he fetched a bucket, filled it with water and went inside to wake the boys.

●　　　●　　　●

Del Crockett woke, walked to the front window of his shanty and looked outside. He watched as Dutch dunked his head in the horse trough then trudged back to the house with a bucket. He knew the boys were in for a rude wake-up call.

He kind of felt left out, but then he always did. Luke treated him like a brother—hell, better than he treated his brothers—and Dutch treated him the same as he did Luke, but Del knew that, deep down, Dutch did not consider him to be the equal of his sons—not even the good-for-nothing Coy.

Del had spent years trying to win Dutch Crater's respect, and maybe this would be his chance to do it. He wasn't sure that Dutch or the boys were going to be able to kill Rachel when they caught up to her, but he knew he'd be able to do it, even though he loved her.

He figured killing the woman he loved was bound to get him Dutch's respect.

Luke was already awake when Dutch came into the house. Across the room both Sam and Coy were snoring like saws.

"Here," Dutch said, handing Luke the bucket. "Wake your brothers up and let's get going."

"What about breakfast, Pa?" Luke asked. "You didn't eat nothin' last night when you was drinkin'—"

"We'll all get somethin' down at the docks, Luke," Dutch said. "Now wake yer good-fer-nothin' brothers up and let's get goin'."

"Yes, Pa."

Luke turned, took two steps and dumped the entire contents of the water bucket on his brothers . . .

TEN

At breakfast in the hotel dining room, Clint brought up the subject of money.

"Oh God, I'm so sorry," Rachel said. "You must think I'm trying to get out from under my debt. How much do I owe you?"

He told her and she reached into her carpetbag and paid him, handing the money across the table.

"Thanks," he said, tucking the money away.

"Clint," she asked then, "how far are you going on the train?"

"New Mexico," he said. "You'll be getting off before I do."

"I, uh, wanted to talk to you about that," she said. "I'd like to hire you."

"To do what?"

"To accompany me to Texas," she said. "I'm going to need help with . . . with Ethan every step of the way."

"I'm sure you can find some help—"

"You saw how the men on the docks helped me."

"You'll find more courtesy the farther west you get," Clint said.

"Were you in Missouri on a job?"

"Yes, I was."

"So I guess you made enough money to justify coming here?"

Clint hesitated, then said, "No, I didn't. The job . . . went bad."

"So you didn't get paid?"

"I got paid," he said, "just not all that was coming to me."

"Then maybe I can make up the difference."

"I don't think so."

"Why?" she asked. "How much were you supposed to get?"

"Another five thousand."

She sat back in her chair and blinked at him.

"See?" he said. "You don't have that kind of money, do you?"

"Well," she said, "no, but . . ." She hesitated, then picked up her bag and dug through it for a few moments. When she was done, she looked around to see if they were being watched, then pushed some money across the table to him.

"Would three thousand be enough?"

After breakfast Clint went to the back of the hotel and climbed aboard the buckboard. He drove it around to the front, where Rachel was waiting. He got down and helped her up into the seat, tossing her bag into the back with the coffin.

"I just thought of something," she said, before he could climb up next to her.

"What's that?"

"When we get to the train, and we get the coffin loaded, what do we do with the buckboard and horse?"

"I took care of that when I rented them," he said. "I arranged for them to be picked up."

"I like a man who thinks ahead."

Clint climbed up on the seat next to her and gathered up the reins.

He still had not given her an answer to her attempt to hire him. When she'd tried to hand him three thousand dollars, he pushed it back across the table at her.

"Put that away," he'd said.

"I know it's not enough, but—"

"Put it away before someone sees it!" he told her, firmly. Quickly she retrieved the money and put it back in her bag.

"You won't do it?" she asked.

"Let me think about it."

And he still was as they drove away from the hotel to the train station . . .

Magellan saw the buckboard with the coffin pull up in front of the station and watched with interest as the man stepped down. He saw what the dockworkers had meant. This was a man who wore a gun on his hip like he knew how to use it.

Magellan had only seen Rachel once, but he recognized her right away. She was a hard woman to forget.

He tried to make himself blend into the background as he watched the pair.

"Stay here," Clint said. "I'll go and talk to the ticket agent, see if we can get some men to help unload."

"You loaded it by yourself."

"I'm not going to want to carry it to the train alone," he said. "I'd like to have a couple of men do it for me, even if I have to pay them."

"Well, if you do," she said, "come to me for the money. I can pay my own way, you know."

As a matter of fact, he did.

ELEVEN

"You'll have to wait until the train pulls in and then get two men to help you from the baggage car," the ticket clerk said. "That's the best I can do for you, mister."

"All right," Clint said. "Thanks."

"That your buckboard out there with the coffin?"

"That's right."

"Is it ripe yet?" the man asked. "Startin' to smell yet?"

"No, not yet," Clint said. "The train will have a cold car, won't it?"

"I hope so," the clerk said, "but it seems to me that at some point you're gonna have to deal with the smell."

"Then we'll deal with it when the time comes," Clint said. He didn't want to admit that he had not even considered it until now, when the clerk mentioned it. What was he thinking—and what was she thinking—would happen when the coffin sat out in the sun a little bit longer? What was she going to do it in Texas, when they off-loaded it into a buckboard and she had to drive it the rest of the way to get where she was going? Had she even thought about the smell?

"Thanks," Clint said to the clerk, and stepped outside.

He stopped short when he saw a tall man in black standing by the buckboard, looking up at Rachel, talking to her. An admirer, or was she already trying to hire someone else?

• • •

45

"Hello, Rachel."

She looked down into the face of a total stranger, but she knew he was trouble as soon as she saw him.

"I don't know you," she said.

"I know you."

Magellan had waited until Clint was inside the terminal, talking to the clerk, before he approached her.

"I don't think you do."

"Come on, Rachel," Magellan said. "It's time to go back."

She turned her head and looked up onto the platform, but did not see Clint yet. All she could think to do was keep the man talking until Clint came back.

"If you don't step away from me, I'll scream," she said.

"Go ahead," he said. "Your friend will come runnin' out and I'll put a bullet in him."

"It won't be that easy."

"I think it will be," Magellan said. "He's a big man, but he looks a bit past it, don't you think?"

"What do you think?" she asked. "You're talkin' about Clint Adams."

Magellan paused.

"That name ring a bell?" she asked.

"It sure does," he said. "I thought I was lucky, findin' you this early in the morning, but Clint Adams, too? This day just gets better and better."

"Good," she said, "a man's last day on earth should be a good one."

"Time to step down from there, Rachel," Magellan said. He reached up and grabbed her arm with his left hand. When he squeezed, pain shot up her arm and he would have dragged her from the buckboard easily, except for one thing.

"Let the lady go!"

As Clint approached the buckboard, he saw the man reach out and grab Rachel's arm. It was obvious from the way she flinched that he was hurting her. Clint quickened his step.

"Let the lady go!" he said, even before he'd reached them.

The man in black turned his head, saw Clint and smiled. But he did release Rachel's arm before stepping away from the buckboard.

"Just invitin' the lady to step down."

"Doesn't look to me like she wants to accept your invitation, fella," Clint said. "Time for you to be on your way."

"I don't think so."

The two men stood and studied each other. Each recognized the other for what he was, a man who lived by the gun—only Clint had been doing it a whole lot longer, and he'd faced a lot of these younger men over the years—in fact, two just yesterday.

Was it only yesterday morning he'd killed those two men in St. Charles?

Rachel watched as the two men faced off. She knew her whole future was now in the hands of Clint Adams. She'd recognized his name from the start, knew who he was, even though she had not let on. From the start she had been unable to believe her luck that Clint Adams—the Gunsmith—had stopped to help her on the dock. Her plan had immediately become to get him to help her take the coffin to Texas. To this point, her plan had worked well. He'd turned down the three thousand at breakfast, but she thought that he would eventually come around and take it, even if she had to use more than money to get him to do so.

Now, though, it all came down to this moment. She didn't know Magellan, but figured she knew who'd sent him.

This was actually her first trial in her quest to get to West Texas with the coffin, and she waited tensely for the outcome.

TWELVE

"What's your name?" Clint asked.

"Magellan."

"Quite a name."

"What's wrong with it?"

"Nothing's wrong with it," Clint said. "It's just a tough name to live up to."

The man obviously knew nothing of the history of his name. It was unlikely he was a descendant of the famous explorer, which pleased Clint. He wouldn't have wanted to terminate such a rich bloodline.

The other thing he found interesting was that the man knew who Clint was.

"You're a famous man," Magellan said, "but I think your best days are behind you, don't you?"

"I guess that's going to be for you to find out."

Magellan was ignoring Rachel, keeping his eyes on Clint. The man might have been past it, but he'd been doing this for a long time, so he was not someone to be taken lightly.

But Megellan was damn sure he could take him.

"Magellan," Clint said, "turn around and walk away and let us get on with our morning."

"Sorry, Adams," the man said, "but that's not doable. I got

49

a job to do, and if I have to go through you to do it, that's what I'm gonna do."

Clint didn't need trouble with the law right now, as he was looking to get on the next train out of Missouri. But he wasn't about to back away from this man, either.

"Let's get it done, then," Clint said. "I've got a train to catch."

"You're not gonna make—"

"Stop talking and do it!" Clint shouted.

Rachel jerked when Clint shouted and almost pulled her derringer from her garter. She kept her hand on the little gun, though, because if Magellan killed Clint, she was going to have to kill him. If, on the other hand, Clint killed the gunman, then he was certainly the man she was looking for.

Magellan flinched at the sound of Clint's voice, and immediately felt foolish and angry about it. It caused him to go for his gun just a little before he was ready, and that cost him . . .

Clint knew he'd startled Magellan into a premature move and he killed the man without compunction. If he hadn't, somebody would have, and soon. Magellan looked the part, but the man was in the wrong business if he could be spooked into a move.

Clint shot Magellan in the chest before the man could get his gun out. The shocked look on the gunman's face said it all, and then his face went blank and he fell over backward, hitting the ground with an audible thud.

"Thank God!" Rachel Chandler said, taking her hand away from her own gun.

THIRTEEN

The law appeared in the person of two uniformed policemen, and Clint gave up his gun upon their request. They escorted both him and Rachel into the waiting room, and they all waited there for a superior officer.

"This is going to make us miss our train," Rachel said, as they waited.

"Maybe not," Clint said. "A superior will be able to make a decision on the spot, and he might actually want us to get on the train."

"I hope so."

"Well," Clint said, "I don't hear a whistle yet. Just let me do the talking, unless you're asked a direct question, okay?"

"I don't know," Rachel said. "Are you workin' for me?"

"Rachel . . ."

"If you were workin' for me, I'd tell the police anythin' you wanted me to."

"Rachel—" Clint started, but he stopped when a man wearing a brown suit and a bowler entered the terminal and stopped to talk to the two uniformed men.

The man turned his head to look at Clint and Rachel, and then started walking over to them.

"Don't play games, Rachel," Clint said, "or neither one of us will be getting on that train."

● ● ● ●

51

Lieutenant Paul Tyler was not happy about being called to the railroad station this early in the morning—especially not to look at a dead body.

"Know him?" he asked the uniformed man who was standing by the body.

"No, sir."

Tyler leaned over the body to get a look at the face.

"Magellan," he said. "Somebody finally killed him." He straightened. "Who did it?"

"Fella in the train station."

"Who's in there with him?"

"Stark and Hutchinson . . . They were the first ones here . . . and there's a woman."

"This was over a woman?" Tyler asked.

The policeman shrugged.

"All right, stay with the body."

"Yes, sir."

Tyler mounted the platform and entered the waiting room. Stark and Hutchinson greeted him and told them their story.

"We got here, one man was dead, and the other was holdin' a gun," Stark said.

"Where's the gun?"

"I have it, sir."

"Let me see it."

Stark removed the gun from his belt and handed it over. Tyler turned it over in his hands, paying special attention to the special grip indentations in the handle.

"Custom made," he said. "This guy's good."

"Had to be good to take Magellan," Hutchinson said.

"Naw," Tyler said, "Magellan wasn't that good. But this fella, he sure is."

"You can tell that from a gun?"

"Do you see this gun?" Tyler asked.

Both men nodded, but looked puzzled.

"Did you ask him his name?"

"Well . . . no," Stark said. "We just took his gun and put him in here with the woman."

Tyler looked over at the man and woman seated together on a bench.

"He gave you his gun, didn't he?"

"Huh?" Stark asked.

"You didn't take it from him. He gave it to you, right?" the lieutenant asked.

"Well . . . right," Hutchinson said.

"His name's Clint Adams."

"How do you know that?' Stark asked.

"This gun belongs to the Gunsmith," Tyler said.

"The Gunsmith?" Stark asked, his face going pale.

"Wow," Hutchinson said.

"So you see," Tyler said, "you couldn't have taken his gun unless he wanted to give it to you."

"God . . . ," Stark said.

"All right," Tyler said, tucking the gun into his own belt, "you fellas can go outside and see that Magellan's body is picked up."

"Yes, sir," Stark said. Both men hurried from the station, glad that their superior had not asked them to stay and help. Not with the Gunsmith. You just didn't run into Western legends like him in St. Louis—not usually—and they weren't happy about the fact that, today, they had.

They would just as soon spend the time outside with the dead body of Frank Magellan.

FOURTEEN

Clint and Rachel both stood as the man in the bowler approached them.

"Mr. Adams?" he asked.

"That's right."

"And the lady?"

"Rachel Chandler," she said.

"Pleased to meet you. My name is Lieutenant Tyler. Seems we had some excitement here this morning."

"Seems so."

"Did either of you know the deceased?" Tyler asked.

"No," Clint said, and Rachel allowed the answer to stand for her, as well.

"I take it the two of you are traveling together?"

"We're taking the same train," Clint said.

"We have a witness who said you arrived at the station together," Tyler said.

Clint figured the only witness could be the ticket clerk, who also saw them together the day before.

"That's right," Clint said, "but we only met yesterday."

"Why don't we all sit down?" Tyler asked. "I'd like you to tell me the conditions of your meeting, and how it all led up to what happened here this morning."

By "why don't we all sit," he meant Clint and Rachel, for

as they sat, he remained standing, looming over them. Clint just figured it was an interrogation technique.

"We met on the docks . . . ," he started.

"So even though you are traveling on the same train," Tyler said, "you still maintain that you are not traveling together?"

"That's right," Clint said.

"Mrs. Chandler, can you tell me what happened with Frank Magellan?"

"He approached me and was makin' rude remarks," she said. "He grabbed my arm, and then Mr. Adams stepped in."

"And that's all there was to it?" the policeman asked.

"That's all."

Tyler scratched his cheek with one fingernail, a curiously delicate gesture.

"Mr. Adams, did Magellan know who you were?"

"Yes, he did," Clint said. "He called me by name."

"And did you tell him Clint's name, ma'am?"

"No, I didn't."

"Then . . . ," he looked at Clint again, "he just recognized you."

"Apparently," Clint said. "His eyes lit up when he saw me. I think he figured on increasing his reputation—or making one for himself, if he didn't have one."

"Oh, he had one," Tyler said, "but it was nothing like yours."

"You recognize me, then?" Clint asked.

"Oh yes," Tyler said. "In fact, I recognized your gun . . . which you might as well have back, by the way."

Tyler removed the gun from his belt and handed it back to Clint, who accepted it, checked to make sure it was still loaded, and then holstered it.

"It's loaded," Tyler said. "None of us fiddled with it. It's quite a weapon, by the way."

"Thanks," Clint said. "Just why are you giving it back to me?"

"I like your story," Tyler said. "Seems to me Magellan was attracted to Miss Chandler—"

"Mrs.," Rachel corrected.

"I'm sorry," Tyler said with a slight bow, "Mrs. Chandler . . . seems he was attracted to her, made his play, then lucked out when he ran into you. Unfortunately for him, it turned out to be bad luck."

"Then we can leave town?" Clint asked.

"By all means," Tyler said. "Mrs. Chandler, is that Mr. Chandler in the coffin?"

"Yes, it is."

"You have my sympathies. How far are you taking him, uh, it?"

"Texas."

"And how far are you going, Mr. Adams?"

"New Mexico, Lieutenant," Clint said. "I'm going home."

At that point they all heard a train whistle in the distance.

"She's on her way in," the ticket clerk sang out. "Better get on the platform."

"Well," Tyler said, "I don't see any reason to detain you."

Clint was surprised.

"Really?" he asked. "No inquest, or statement—"

"Oh, you both just made statements," Tyler said. "I'll write them up when I get back to headquarters."

"That's very nice of you, Lieutenant," Rachel said.

"Not at all, Mrs. Chandler," Tyler said. "I will just sleep better knowing that The Gunsmith is no longer in St. Louis."

"But . . . this wasn't his fault," she argued.

"Forget it, Rachel," Clint said. "I know just what the lieutenant means."

"I thought you would," Tyler said. "I hope you both have a wonderful trip."

"Thank you, Lieutenant." Clint took Rachel's arm. "We'd better get out on the platform."

As they approached the door, Tyler called out, "Will you be needing help with the coffin? I'd be happy to have two of my men assist you."

Clint stopped, turned and said, "Much obliged, Lieutenant. That *would* be a great help."

When the coffin had been loaded onto the refrigerated car— surrounded by a shipment of fresh vegetables—Clint joined Rachel in the passenger car.

"That wasn't very fair," she said, as the train pulled out of the station.

"What wasn't?" Clint asked.

"That policeman sounded like he was blaming you for what happened."

"That's the way it always is, Rachel," Clint said. "It's the man with the bigger reputation who gets blamed for the ruckus."

"How do you live with that?"

"I don't have much of a choice in the matter."

FIFTEEN

The riverboat *Robert E. Lee* pulled in at around eleven A.M., with Coy and Sam Crater just about hanging off the sides.

"I love riverboat rides," Sam said.

"Me, too," Coy agreed.

"And I like St. Louis," Sam said. "Lots to do."

"Not thanks to Billy," Coy said. "With him dead, we ain't here to have fun. The St. Louis women are gonna have to do without ol' Coy and Sam Crater."

"What are you two yappin' about?" Del asked, sidling up next to them and leaning on the rail.

"Stupid Billy gettin' killed," Coy said.

"That's no way to talk about you dead brother," Del warned. "Don't let your pa hear ya."

"I won't," Coy said. "Billy was Pa's baby. He'd whip my ass if he heard me."

Sam chuckled.

"What's so funny?" Coy asked.

"He whipped your ass good yesterday."

"He did not," Coy said. "He got in a lucky punch."

"Don't let him hear you say that, either," Del said.

"I ain't afraid—"

"Quiet," Del said, "here comes him and Luke."

"Ain't we docked yet?" Dutch complained.

"They're just tyin' us off now, Dutch," Del said.

"Let's get down there, then," Dutch said. "We probably missed more than one train, already."

Sam nudged Coy and said, "I like train rides almost as much as riverboat rides."

"Me, too," Coy said.

Coy, Sam and Del waited outside while Dutch and Luke went into the train station to talk to the clerk. When they came out, Dutch's face was bright red.

"We missed them," he said. "They were on the first train of the day."

"The clerk remembered that?" Sam asked.

"What man wouldn't remember Rachel?" Coy asked.

"Shut up!" Dutch said.

"She had the coffin with her," Luke said, "and a man helpin' her."

"Who was the man?" Del asked.

"The clerk didn't know, but he said he killed somebody for her, right here, this mornin'. The police were here."

"Tyler," Dutch said.

"You want me to go talk to him?" Del asked.

"Yeah," Dutch said. "You and Luke find the lieutenant and find out what happened here today."

"Right, Pa," Luke said. He and Del left on foot.

"Whataya want us to do, Pa?" Coy asked.

"We're gonna need money for train tickets, and travelin'," Dutch said. "Go and get some."

"From where?" Sam asked.

Coy nudged his brother to shut up, but it was too late.

"Goddamn it!" Dutch snapped. "Do I have to tell you everythin'? Rob somethin'!"

"Right, Pa," Coy said. "We'll take care of it."

"Coy!"

"Yeah, Pa?"

"I said rob someplace," Dutch said, "but don't you kill nobody. We don't need that kinda heat, right now."

"Gotcha, Pa."

With that Coy and Sam went off to do one of their favorite things—terrorize someone, and rob them.

Dutch sat down on a bench on the platform, crossed one knee over the other and settled in to wait. In his mind he went over several different ways he thought he could take revenge for Billy's death.

SIXTEEN

Once they were on the train, Clint said to Rachel, "You want to tell me about it?"

"About what?"

"What happened back there."

"You were there," she said. "You saw what happened. That man got fresh with me and then you killed him."

"I killed him because he tried to kill me," Clint said, "not because he got fresh with you. He didn't give me any other choice."

"Well, what do you want me to tell you?"

"He knew my name," Clint said. "Did you tell him?"

"The lieutenant asked me that and I answered it," she said.

"Now answer it for me."

"I did not tell him who you were."

"So he just recognized me."

"Apparently," she said. "Aren't you used to being recognized?"

"By name, yes," Clint said, "but not so much on sight."

They rode in silence for a while and then he asked, "So you didn't know who I was when I introduced myself?"

"I knew you were Clint Adams," she said. "That's all. I didn't know anything about a reputation until you and that man talked, and then the lieutenant mentioned it." She turned in her window seat to look at him. "What's this about?"

"I'm just wondering, is all," he said.

"Wondering what?"

"If you're telling me everything."

"And just what is it I wouldn't be telling you?"

"Well," he said, "what's actually in that coffin, for one thing."

"We can go back and take a look now," she said, "if you want to put your mind at ease."

He thought about it for a moment, but if there was not a body in that box, would she be inviting him to have a look?

"No," he said, "I believe there's a body in there, but what else might there be?"

She hesitated, then said, "All right, I'll tell you. My husband had some jewelry he wanted to be buried with."

"Jewelry?"

"Some rings, a watch, cuff links, a tie pin . . . all these things have diamonds in them."

"And they're worth money?"

"Quite a bit."

"Why would you bury all that jewelry with him?"

"I told you," she answered. "He wanted to be buried with it."

"But you could use the money you might get from selling it, couldn't you?"

"I have some money."

"I meant more than the money you tried to give me."

"I have more than three thousand dollars, Clint," she said, "just not on me. Is that what this is about? You want me to offer you more money?"

"No," he said, "that's not what it's about. It's about me killing a man and not knowing why."

"And that bothers you?"

"You're damned right it does."

"Well," she said, "if it's any consolation to you, I'm sorry you had to kill him because of me."

He leaned his head back and closed his eyes.

"I guess it wasn't you fault," he conceded. "He asked for it."

"Yes," she said, "he did, and you shouldn't feel badly about it."

"Sure," he said.

It got quiet then, and he assumed she had also closed her

eyes and put her head back. Several minutes later, however, she spoke again.

"Will this train take me right to Texas?"

"No," he said, "you'll have to make a switch at Oklahoma City." He opened his eyes and looked at her. "I never asked you what part of Texas you're going to."

"Austin."

"You've got a long way to go," he said.

"I know."

"How do you expect—" He stopped short, not wanting to upset her.

"What is it?" she asked. "What do you want to ask me?"

"How do you expect to get the body all the way there without some . . . deterioration?"

"Are you concerned that the body might start to smell?"

"Well . . . yes."

"I was hoping there'd be some refrigerated cars all the way."

"Lucky for you there probably will be," he said. "But what if you ended up having to spend some time on the trail, with the coffin in back of a buckboard?"

"Well, I guess I should have told you," she replied. "The body was embalmed before I left."

"I see."

"That should help it keep longer, shouldn't it?"

"Probably," he said. "I'm no undertaker."

"Have you made up your mind yet?"

"About what?"

"Whether or not you're going to help me get my husband to Austin."

"It's a long way to go."

"For three thousand dollars?"

He put his head back again and closed his eyes.

"I still have some time to think about it," he said.

SEVENTEEN

Luke and Del were the first ones to return to the train station.

"What did Tyler have to say for himself?" Dutch asked.

"He said he just wanted to get Clint Adams out of St. Louis," Luke said.

"He said we should know who Clint Adams is, Dutch," Del said. "Do you know?"

"God," Dutch said, "just because you're young don't mean you got to be stupid. Tyler didn't tell you?"

"He said you'd tell us," Luke said. "Who is he, Pa?"

"He's the Gunsmith," Dutch said. "That name make a dent in your thick skulls?"

"The Gunsmith?" Luke asked.

"Ain't he an old gunman?" Del asked.

"Not so old," Dutch said. "Probably about my age."

"How did Rachel get a gunman to help her?" Luke wondered.

"How else?" Dutch asked. "With money."

"You think she hired herself a gun?" Luke asked.

"Ain't it obvious?" Dutch asked.

"So what do we do?" Luke asked.

"We're goin' after them," Dutch said. "I got tickets for all of us on the next train."

"But where she goin', Pa?" Luke asked. "We don't even know."

"Yeah, we do." Del said.

"Tell him, Del."

Luke looked at Del.

"Texas," Del said, "she's goin' to Texas."

"And we're goin' after her," Dutch said. "Now, if your idiot brothers would just get back with the money, we can pay for these tickets."

There was enough room for Rachel to get up and leave her seat without disturbing Clint, who was dozing with his head back. She walked to the back of the car, left, went through the next car and kept going until she came to the refrigerated car. She found a conductor and told the man she had to get into the car.

"We're really not supposed to open that car until we get to our destination, ma'am." He said. "It could ruin the vegetables."

"Sir, I just have to get back there and talk to my husband," she said. "I know it sounds silly to you"—she touched his arm, because she knew she could get men to do what she wanted by doing this—"but I just need a few minutes." Now a tear—just one, squeezed out so it would roll down her pale cheek.

The conductor, a man in is forties, was ill equipped to deal with this kind of persuasion, and finally gave in.

"Oh, thank you, sir."

He unlocked the door and allowed her to enter the car . . .

Clint felt and heard Rachel get up and leave, because after all these years he did not sleep soundly—ever. He waited until she was gone, then opened his eyes, stood up and followed her. He watched as she worked on the conductor, and then as she entered the refrigerated car. When she came back out, she touched the conductor's arm again and said something that made the man blush. Clint turned and walked back to his seat, and had his eyes closed when Rachel returned and sat down. A half an hour later he heard her breathing become even and regular and knew she was asleep. He stood up, left the car and found that same conductor . . .

"Sir, I can't do that," the conductor said.

"Sure, you can," Clint said. "You just let the lady go in."

"Sir," the conductor said, "that's her husband in that coffin, and she needed to, uh, talk to him."

"Now that she's not here, standing in front of you," Clint said, "touching you and crying, that sounds kind of silly, doesn't it?"

Looking embarrassed, the conductor said, "Yeah, it does."

"Okay," Clint said, "I need to get into that car for just a few minutes, and I've only got two things to offer you to let me in."

"Uh, w-what—"

"This," Clint said, showing the man some money, "or this," he said, indicating the gun on his hip.

The conductor was also ill equipped to handle these forms of persuasion, but he went for the money and unlocked the door.

"Smart man," Clint said.

He went inside and immediately saw his breath. It was cold inside, but he only needed a few minutes. He approached the coffin and grasped the ends of the lid. When it didn't give, he ran his hands over the lid and found some nails that he thought could be removed, but he would need a hammer or another tool. Could Rachel have opened the coffin while she was here?

He walked around the coffin, brushing by a bushel of lettuce as he did so. Running his hands along the sides and the bottoms, he could not find a way to easily get into the box. His hands were starting to feel like ice, so he gave up and left the car.

"May I lock it now?" the conductor asked.

"Sure, lock it."

The conductor did so, then turned to Clint and asked, "Are you the deceased's brother?"

"No."

"Friend?"

"You could say that."

"He must have been a very nice man."

"He was a prince," Clint said. "Thanks. Oh, one more thing."

"Yes?"

"Mrs. Chandler is not to know that I went in there. Do you understand?"

"Yes, sir," the man said. "In fact, she told me the same thing about you."

"That's fine," Clint said. "Just forget this ever happened and we'll all get along."

"Yes, sir," the conductor said. "I'll do that."

Rachel felt Clint Adams return to his seat. She gave him enough time to get comfortable, then opened her eyes to look at him. His head was back and he seemed to be dozing. She knew that even if he had gone into the refrigerated car, he would not have been able to get the coffin open.

She smiled to herself, put her own head back and, this time, actually did drift off to sleep.

EIGHTEEN

By the time it was dark out, they were both awake—or, at least, both had ceased trying to pretend to be asleep.

"How fast are we going?" Rachel asked, looking out into the dark.

"I think the steam engine can get up to twenty or twenty-five miles an hour," Clint said. "Those are the passenger trains. The freight trains do about ten to twelve."

"We're carrying freight and passengers," she pointed out.

"Then I vote for fifteen to eighteen miles an hour."

"God, it'll take forever to get to Texas."

"Longer than forever," Clint said. "Like I said, you're going to have to change trains in Oklahoma City. It'll take us about twenty-five hours to get just that far."

She hesitated for a moment, then said, "I have to buy some new clothes."

"What?"

"New clothes," she said. "I only have a few changes. I'm going to need some new clothes."

Clint stared at her. At his age he'd long ago decided he didn't understand women, and Rachel was doing nothing to change his mind.

Since they had to wait for a train, Dutch decided to send some telegrams.

71

"We got family all over the West," he told the boys. "All we got to do is get them all involved."

"Doin' what?" Coy asked.

"Checkin' trains," Dutch said.

"But . . . where?" Sam asked.

"Texas, for one, but the ticket clerk told me there are some stops in Oklahoma."

"Oklahoma City," Del said. They all looked at him. "If she's gonna take a train into Texas, she'll probably have to get it there."

"That's good thinkin'," Dutch said. "I'm sure we can cover Oklahoma City and Austin."

As Dutch went back into the train station, where there was a telegraph key, Coy asked, "Who do we know in Oklahoma City and Austin?"

"Uncle Roy, in Oklahoma City," Luke said. "He was Ma's brother."

"And Cousin Floyd, in Austin," Del said.

"Cousin?" Sam asked.

"Distant cousin," Del said.

"How do you know about our cousin?" Coy asked, belligerently.

"I heard Dutch talkin' about him, once," Del said. "Floyd Crater."

Coy resented the fact that, sometimes, Del Crockett seemed to know more about the Crater family than he did.

"That train clerk ain't gonna let Pa use the telegraph in there," Sam predicted.

"How much you want to bet?" Luke asked.

"Sir, I can't let you use this key," the man said. "It's railroad property."

"Friend, I don't want to use it—"

"Well, that's good—"

"I want you to use it and send the message like I tell it to you," Dutch said.

"I can't do that."

"Why not?" Dutch asked. "It's railroad property, and you work for the railroad."

"But it's not railroad business."

"It could be," Dutch said.

The clerk looked puzzled and asked, "How?"

Dutch took out his gun, pointed it at the man and cocked the hammer back.

"You could send a message that they need to replace you."

"Did you send the telegrams?" Luke asked, as Dutch returned to them on the platform.

"Yeah," Dutch said.

Luke held out his hand and Sam gave him two bits.

"What was that for?" Dutch asked.

"Sam bet me the clerk wouldn't let you use the telegraph key," Luke explained.

Dutch looked at Sam.

"You was wrong," he said. "The clerk was very helpful."

Sam made a face, but it changed when they all heard a train whistle in the distance.

"Is that the train?" Coy asked.

Dutch looked at his son sadly, and shook his head, exchanging a glance with Luke.

"No, you idiot," Dutch said, "that's a goddamn railroad bird."

Coy frowned, then the light dawned and he said, "Ah, there ain't no such thing."

"Bright boy," Dutch said.

NINETEEN

By the time the sun came up the next morning, they were about five hours from Oklahoma City.

"God," Rachel said, stretching, "every muscle hurts."

Clint had been awake most of the night, which had been oddly surreal, as everyone else in the car had been asleep, including Rachel. He'd studied her profile in repose, and realized she really was quite beautiful. Still, that had no effect on his final decision about whether or not to accompany her—and her coffin—to Texas.

"I've got to stretch my legs," she said, standing up. "Would you like to talk a walk?"

Apparently, she wasn't intending to visit the coffin again.

"Sure," he said. "I could use some fresh air."

He stood, and they both walked to the back of the car and stepped outside. As they did so, the conductor came out of the connecting car, saw them and pointedly ignored them both.

"What's his problem?" Rachel wondered, out loud.

"Must have something on his mind."

Rachel took a deep breath with her eyes closed.

"Have you made a decision?" she asked.

He didn't bother pretending he didn't know what she was talking about.

"I have," Clint said. "I'm sorry, but I'm going to have to say no. I'm just going to head home."

75

She folded her arms and said, "All right, I understand. I'll just have to do the best I can."

"Rachel," he said, "you'll be getting off in Oklahoma City. I'm sure you can hire someone to help you, and for a lot less than you offered me."

"I'm sure you're right, Clint," she said. "I'm going to go back to my seat."

He let her go inside alone. Accompanying her to Texas just wasn't high up on his list of things to do, and he had been away from his place for too long, for no reason.

The door opened behind him and the conductor came out again. Clint looked at him, and this time the man gave him a simple nod and kept going.

Clint went back inside, figuring the last few hours of this trip with Rachel were going to be quiet.

He was wrong . . .

By the time the conductor walked through announcing Oklahoma City as the next stop, Rachel had talked nonstop for three hours. The thing was, Clint could not have told anyone what she talked about for all that time. He thought that she was probably nervous about getting off the train alone and that was why she kept talking. He simply nodded and made a comment every once in a while that he thought might be appropriate.

Once the conductor made his announcement, she stopped and looked at Clint.

"I'm sorry," she said, "I've talked your ear off for two hours."

"Three," he said, "but it's okay."

"I want to thank you again for the help you've given me," she said. "I don't blame you for not wanting to go all the way to Texas with a coffin and a crazy woman."

"Thanks," he said, choosing not to comment beyond that.

"I guess . . . Do I have to go back to the other car now, or . . . ?" She turned in her seat to look behind them.

"Just get off and they'll help you off-load the . . . your husband, but wait for the train to stop."

"I'm just nervous," she said. "First I couldn't stop talking, and now I'm just jittery."

"You'll be fine," he said.

If she was making one last-ditch effort to persuade him by making him feel guilty, she was out of luck.

Roy Frump watched as the train pulled into the Oklahoma City station, wondering if this was the one. It was the third train to come in from the East since he'd arrived early that morning, and he was getting tired of waiting.

When he'd gotten the telegram from Dutch Crater, he had been tempted to just tear it up and throw it away. He'd never liked his sister's husband, thought that Dutch Crater was a bully. He'd never had a wife and kids of his own, but if he did, he never would have treated them the way Dutch treated his.

Looking at Roy Frump, it wasn't hard to figure out why he'd never married. He was possibly the ugliest man who ever lived, with huge lips and ears and a skinny neck. He seemed to be all arms and legs because he was so thin and tall, and he always wore coveralls with nothing on underneath. People stepped around him or looked away when they saw him, and the only people who ever bothered with him were his friends, Bobo and Keenan. They were brothers Roy had made friends with years ago, and when he had told them he was going to Oklahoma City to do a favor for his brother-in-law, they had insisted on going along with him.

His final decision to agree to help Dutch was made in memory of his sister, whom he loved until the day she died. To this day he'd never met any of his nephews, but since they were all on their way, maybe he'd finally get to see them. He wondered if they favored their ma or their pa.

He sort of hoped they looked like their pa, because the men in his family tended to look like him.

"Here comes a train, Roy," Keenan said.

Keenan did all the talking for him and Bobo, because he was the smart one. He was also the oldest by a few years, and at three hundred pounds, he was about twenty pounds heavier.

Both brothers were bald, though, and few people could tell them apart.

"What do we do now?" Keenan asked.

"We wait," Roy said, around a huge chaw of tobacco. "I don't know what this gal looks like, so we got to wait and see which woman gets off the train with a coffin."

Keenan—the smarter brother—looked at him and asked, "What if there's more than one?"

Roy scratched his head.

"I don't think there'll be two, Keenan," he said, "but if there is, we'll just ask 'em which one is named Rachel."

Keenan looked at Bobo, who nodded.

"Yeah," Keenan said, "that'll work."

TWENTY

"Well," Rachel said, "good-bye."

"Good-bye."

They shook hands briefly, and then Rachel walked to the front of the car and, with the assistance of the conductor, got off the train.

"Thank you," she said to him.

"Any time, ma'am," the conductor said. "If you just walk back to the freight car, they'll help you with your, uh, husband."

She nodded, smiled and walked back. She had to pass the window she'd been sitting at, and saw Clint looking out at her, and she smiled at him, too . . .

Roy, Keenan and Bobo walked along the platform until they saw the car they wanted.

"That'd be it," Roy said. "Let's wait here and see what happens."

All three of them were carrying rifles, and there wasn't a handgun between them.

They watched a woman walk up to the car, talk to two men who then went inside and reappeared, carrying a pine coffin.

"That's her," Roy said. "Let's go."

Rachel watched as the two men lowered the coffin to the ground, one outside the car and one still inside. Then the man

79

inside dropped to the ground and the two of them lifted the coffin up onto the platform.

"That's as far as we go, ma'am," one of them said. "You got someone to help you?"

"I'll find someone," she said. "Thanks."

She had been sure she could convince Clint Adams to help her, but he'd seemed immune to the ways she usually got men to do what she wanted them to do. He was an unusual man, helping her for his own reasons, and now not helping her in the same way.

"Good luck, ma'am."

"Thanks."

She turned and saw the three men in overalls coming toward her purposefully. Before she could say anything, they were on her, one of them—the tall, skinny, ugly one—grabbing her by the arm.

"Hey, Rachel," he said to her, "Dutch told us to say hello."

"Wha—"

"You're comin' with us."

Roy grabbed Rachel's arm and pulled her away from the coffin. Keenan and Bobo picked up the coffin and followed behind.

"Wait," Rachel said. "What are you doing? Who are you?"

"We're family, Rachel," Roy said. "Dutch sent us a message to meet you at the train."

"You can't do this," she said, trying to dig her heels in.

Only a few other people had gotten off the train, so there was no one in their way as Roy continued to drag Rachel along, the brothers following with the coffin.

"Oh my God," she said, realizing what was happening. Dutch had sent a message ahead, and now they had her. "No. No!"

As the train started to pull away, Clint looked out the window again, just in time to catch the scene: one man holding Rachel's arm, obviously dragging her, while two other men—big men, but not fat—followed, carrying the coffin effortlessly between them.

It wasn't his business, he told himself. He'd taken her as

far as he could—but what good was seeing her this far if she wasn't going to get any farther

"Goddamnit!" he said, rushing to the front of the car before the train got up too much speed.

TWENTY-ONE

Oddly, as Clint dropped down from the moving train to the platform, he thought he was going to have to buy all new clothes, because he was leaving any belongings that weren't on his person behind. All he had was his gun, and that was co-incidentally what he needed right at that moment.

The three men had not yet gotten Rachel—and the coffin—off the platform, and as the train rumbled by, Clint called out to her. Neither she nor the men heard him, however, because of the noise, so he started running down the platform toward them. They were heading away from him, so the one he could see most clearly was the big man carrying the back end of the coffin.

Just as the last car of the train left the station, Clint reached that man and did the only thing he could think of to get his attention short of shooting him—he tripped him.

The man stumbled and released the back of the coffin. The box struck the platform with a bang as the big fella righted himself before falling and turned to glare at Clint.

In Bobo's little brain a spark went off that told him not to fall, but it was mostly instinct that held him up. When he turned to look at whoever had tripped him, it was more with hurt feelings than anything else, for Bobo was as gentle as a lamb unless he was told not to be.

• • •

"Wha—" Keenan felt the weight of the coffin shift, dragging his arm down, and he turned to see what had happened. He saw Bobo facing another man on the platform, and he knew the other man must have done something to his brother, because carrying the coffin was child's play for both of them. There was no way Bobo would have dropped it otherwise.

"What the hell—" he said, finishing his original thought.

And then suddenly it was quiet.

Keenan shouted, "Roy!"

"What?" Roy turned at the sound of his name and saw the brothers facing a man on the platform.

"What the hell—" he said. "You fellas can't carry a little coffin without droppin' it?"

"He made Bobo drop it," Keenan said, pointing to Clint.

"Who the hell are you?" Roy said.

"Clint!" Rachel shouted. "Thank God."

"Clint?" Roy said. "Who the hell is Clint?"

Rachel, now that she wasn't being dragged, reached beneath her skirt with her free hand.

"Let her go," Clint Adams said.

The big man he'd tripped had held onto his rifle, and the other two men also had a rifle in one hand.

"What?"

"Who's he?" Keenan asked.

"Never mind who I am," Clint said. "The lady obviously doesn't want to go with you, so let her go."

"Mister," Roy said, "this here's family business, so you better butt out."

"What family?" Clint asked. "Is she your family?"

"I am not!" Rachel shouted, before Roy could answer.

"Keenan," Roy said, "you and Bobo kill that son of a bitch."

"Right, Roy."

Bobo reacted immediately to the order, bringing his rifle up to point it at Clint. Without hesitating, Clint drew his gun and fired. The bullet struck Bobo in the chest, but the man was so big it seemed to hardly effect him. It did, however, cause him to lower the barrel of his rifle.

Behind him Keenan started bringing his rifle up.

"Don't!" Clint shouted, but the man was beyond caring what Clint had to say.

Clint had no choice. He fired, putting a bullet in Keenan's chest, but as with his brother, it seemed to have hardly any effect.

So he shot them both again.

He fired a second time at Bobo, and a red hole appeared in his forehead. Likewise, he sent a chunk of lead into Keenan's brain by way of his forehead. Both men fell, with Keenan actually tumbling off the platform and onto the tracks.

Roy had continued on, assuming that Keenan and Bobo would do what he'd told them to do.

"Stop right there!" Clint shouted.

Roy turned, an annoyed look on his face, which turned to astonishment as he saw the only two friends he had in the world lying dead. He released Rachel's arm. In that moment Rachel brought her other hand up, pressed the barrel of her derringer to Roy's temple and fired.

The man jerked, seemed to shudder, and then his legs folded beneath him and he fell facedown onto the platform.

TWENTY-TWO

Clint checked Bobo and Roy to be sure they were dead. Down on the tracks Keenan wasn't moving, and was obviously as dead as the others.

"What did you do—" he started to ask Rachel, but then he saw the derringer in her hand.

"How long have you had that?" he asked.

"Years," she said, lifting her skirt and replacing the gun. When she straightened, she said, "Your train is gone."

"Yeah," he said, "with my saddlebags."

He ejected the spent shells from his gun, reloaded and slid the weapon home into its holster.

"Okay," he said, "before the law shows up, tell me who these men were."

"I don't know who they were," she said. "They just grabbed me and Ethan, and started carrying us off."

"Without a word?"

"Yes," she said. "I kept asking who they were, but they wouldn't answer me."

"The skinny one said something about family business," Clint said. "What do you suppose he meant by that?"

"I don't know," she said. "Maybe they were brothers?"

"Maybe those two were," Clint said, "but not him."

"Well, I don't know," she said. "I just know I'm in your debt—again."

"Well, you took care of him pretty well without me."

"I doubt my gun would have stopped those two," she said. "Besides, I only had one other shot."

Clint looked up and down the platform. If there were any other people there, they had taken cover when the shooting started. He turned and looked at the coffin, which seemed no worse for wear.

"Ethan looks okay," he said.

"Clint," she said, "I don't know what to do. It seems obvious to me, with what happened in St. Louis and now here, that somebody doesn't want me to get to Texas."

"Yeah," he said, "it seems pretty obvious to me, too. These two incidents can't be coincidence—but who could that someone be?"

"I don't know!" she said.

"Did you husband have enemies?"

"Even if he did," she said, "he's dead now. Why would they want his body?"

"Or his wife?"

She shrugged her arms helplessly.

"They seem to be anticipating where you're going," he said.

"So they'll be waiting the next time I get off a train, as well?" she asked.

"Only if you take a train again."

"Well, what else—"

"Wait."

Some men mounted the platform at the far end, behind Rachel, and were coming toward them. They wore blue uniforms and badges, and Clint had a feeling they were a combination of city police and railroad security.

"All right," he said, "let me do the talking as much as possible, all right?"

"Sure," she said. "I think I know how to do that."

As the men reached them, Clint raised his arms away from his gun. One of the men in blue snatched it from his holster while the others held their guns on him.

"You all right, ma'am?" one of them asked.

"Yes, I am."

"This feller attack you?"

"No," she said, "they did. He saved me."

The policemen looked down at the dead men, and then back at Clint.

"I think we all better wait for our boss to show up," one policeman said.

"And mine," said the railroad man.

"Why don't we wait inside?" Clint asked. "The lady would like to sit down."

"Oh, that's all right," Rachel said, lowering herself onto the coffin. "I can sit right here."

TWENTY-THREE

The supervisor of the uniformed police introduced himself as Sergeant Dan Tanner. Like the lieutenant in St. Louis, he wore a suit and tie and hat. He appeared to be in his mid-thirties, and Clint could see the bulge of his gun beneath his arm.

Ed Morgan was the head of the railroad security, and his men called him "Cap'n." He was older than Tanner, almost fifty, and he glared at Clint from behind a huge unlit cigar.

The third man to arrive was Sheriff Carl Brody, a fortyish, hangdog-looking man who didn't seem to want to be left out of the festivities.

All of them men treated Rachel with respect and deference, and eyed Clint with suspicion, especially after he identified himself.

"Clint Adams?" the sheriff asked. "You mean . . . the Gunsmith?"

"You know this fella?" the younger police sergeant asked.

"Doesn't everybody?" the railroad captain asked.

"Well, I don't," Tanner said. "So somebody fill me in so I don't feel left out."

Since Tanner worked for the city police, he seemed to be the man with the most authority, even though he was the youngest of the three. Still, Clint decided to direct most of his attention to the sheriff, in the hopes of getting this business over with as soon as possible.

However, he left it up to someone else to fill the policeman in on who he was.

To that end, the railroad bull, Captain Morgan, pulled Tanner aside and began to talk to him urgently, in low tones.

"The sergeant is from the East," Sheriff Brody said. "Very often he needs to be filled in on things we all already know."

"He's lucky to have such helpful friends," Rachel said.

"Sheriff," Clint offered, "those men didn't give me much choice in the matter. They were manhandling Mrs. Chandler, hustling her off the platform against her will. All I did was call them on it and they started shooting."

"I wasn't aware they'd fired any shots," Brody said.

"They were about to," Clint said. "They were bringing their rifles to bear."

"I know these boys," Brody said. "Keenan and Bobo didn't usually kill anyone unless they were told to."

"They were," Rachel said, speaking up despite her agreement to let Clint do the talking. "That other man told them to kill Clint."

"I see," Brody said. "And Mrs. Chandler, the bullet that was fired into Roy Frump's skull doesn't appear to have come from Clint's infamous gun. Can you explain that?"

"I carry a derringer for protection, Sheriff," she said. "This seemed like a good opportunity to use it."

"You're probably right about that."

"Do you have any witnesses to what happened, Sheriff?" Clint asked. "They would support our story."

"Well," the sheriff said, "the two who off-loaded the coffin are gone, of course, havin' left with the train. We do have one or two people who were on the platform, but they seem to have run for cover before the shots were actually fired."

"All right," Sergeant Tanner said, returning to the group with Cap'n Morgan. "I guess I'm filled in now. Mr. Adams, seems you're some kind of legend of the Old West. Well, I have to tell you, Oklahoma City is not the Old West. We may not be that far from Dodge City and Abilene geographically, but we couldn't be further away in, uh, other ways."

"I understand."

"Do you?" Tanner asked. "Do you really understand that we can't have shots being fired in public places?"

"Believe me, Sergeant," Clint said, "if there had been any other way, I would have taken it."

"Well, you've killed three men in my jurisdiction—"

"Two," Sheriff Brody said.

"What?"

"Two," Brody repeated, "he killed two men. Mrs. Chandler killed the third."

Tanner looked around, but none of his own men were available. He looked at Morgan, who shrugged.

"I checked the bodies when I came in," Brody said. He touched his temple. "Frump has a little hole right here. It's from a two-shot—" He stopped and looked at Rachel. "Two-shot?"

"Yes."

"It's from a two-shot derringer she carries."

Looking confused, Tanner asked, "Where?"

Rachel put her leg up on the bench, pulled her skirt all the way up to reveal a very shapely thigh with a derringer attached, and said, "Right here."

Tanner looked, then quickly blushed and looked away.

"Uh, thank you."

"Don't mention it," Rachel said, letting her skirt drop. Clint noticed that neither Brody nor Morgan was shy about looking at her thigh. He hadn't been particularly shy about it, either.

"Would you, uh, mind telling me where the two of you are headed?" Sergeant Tanner asked.

Rachel looked at Clint expectantly. He sighed and said to the assemblage of law enforcement personnel, "We're headed for Texas."

"Together?" Tanner asked.

"Yes, together."

"So you'll be wanting to take the next train out?"

"No," Clint said. "We'll be wanting to rent a couple of horses and a buckboard."

"You're not taking the train?" Morgan asked.

"Sorry, Cap'n," Clint said, "but the train doesn't seem to be a particularly safe mode of transportation for us right now."

He hoped they wouldn't ask for further explanation of that comment, as he didn't really want to fill them in on what happened in St. Louis.

"Well," Tanner said, "if you don't have a train to catch, then you won't mind staying in town for another day or so. I'm going to have to go to my superiors with this."

"What for, Tanner?" Sheriff Brody asked. "They were defending themselves. Let them leave, for Chrissake, before someone else tries to kill them."

"That may be the way things were done around here before, Sheriff," Tanner said, "but not anymore. I have superiors to answer to. I can't just arbitrarily rule on a street shooting myself."

Brody gave Clint a look and a shrug that said, *What are you gonna do?*

"It's okay," Clint said, to the sheriff's surprise. "We're going to need time to get outfitted. We probably wouldn't be able to leave until tomorrow, anyway."

"Well, we'll see about that," Sergeant Tanner said. "There's a very good likelihood, Mr. Adams, that I might be forced to arrest you come tomorrow."

Clint looked at Tanner, waiting for what he hoped would not come next.

"In fact," the sergeant said, "I think I'm going to have to ask you for your gun." The man put his hand out.

That was the very comment Clint had been hoping against.

"Don't."

Tanner blinked.

"I'm sorry?"

"Don't ask me for my gun."

"Why not?"

"Because I'd have to refuse," Clint said, "and then you might have to arrest me today."

"See here—" Tanner started, but this time it was Brody who took his arm and pulled him aside, spoke to him urgently and in low tones.

"Why not give him your gun?" Rachel asked.

"Because it's the quickest way for me to end up dead."

They waited a few moments while Brody and Tanner conferred, and then the two men returned.

"All right, Mr. Adams," Tanner said. "The sheriff has convinced me that being seen on the streets of our city without a gun might entice someone to take a shot at you because of your reputation. So I'm going to allow you to keep your weapon."

"That's decent of you."

"I'd like to know what hotel you'll be staying in."

"I don't know," Clint said. "Recommend one."

"I think Mrs. Chandler would enjoy the Continental Hotel. It has the best bath facilities in the city," Sheriff Brody said. "And it's not far from here."

Clint looked at Sergeant Tanner and said, "We'll be at the Continental."

"Very well," Tanner said. "You'll be hearing from me." He then turned to Brody and Morgan. "Do either of you gentlemen have any other questions?"

"I don't," Brody said, and Morgan simply shook his head.

"Mr. Adams," Tanner said, "please do your best not to kill anyone else while you're in Oklahoma City."

"That's not fair," Rachel said. "It wasn't his—"

"That's okay, Rachel," Clint said. "I think it's safe to assure the sergeant that I'll try."

TWENTY-FOUR

The Continental turned out to be one of the more expensive places in town, and even though Clint had most of the original thousand dollars he'd been paid by Devlin, he agreed to allow Rachel to pay for both of their rooms.

They also agreed that they would both bathe and then meet for lunch and what Rachel called "a little shopping spree." What she meant, of course, was new clothes, but what it meant to Clint was horses, and a buckboard and other supplies they would need to travel.

The hotel had its own livery, so they were able to safely tuck Ethan's coffin there and not worry about it. At least, Clint didn't worry about it. For all he knew Rachel had snuck down there a couple of times to check on it. He still wished he'd been able to get it open on the train and have a look inside.

They met in the lobby and decided to eat in the hotel dining room, which had all the appearances of a five-star New York restaurant.

"Alton never had a place like this to eat," she said, when they were seated.

"Rachel," he said, "I get the impression you and your husband lived well in Alton."

"As well as you could, there," she said. "But there was nothing like this."

"What about in St. Louis?"

97

"I think I told you once before we didn't go to St. Louis very much," she said. "Ethan didn't like to leave home much."

A waiter come over then and took their orders. Rachel went first and ordered a chicken dish, while Clint stuck with a steak dinner.

"I have to thank you, yet again," she said, over dinner.

"For what?"

"For agreeing to go with me to Texas," she said. "When they asked if we were traveling together, you could have said no."

"I should have said no," he replied, "but my train was gone."

"You're worried about me," she said. "You're a tough man, but you're worried I'll get killed if you don't take me."

"You might still get killed," Clint said, "and me with you." He put his fork down and leaned forward. "Just for the record, Rachel, I still think you're holding out on me."

"About what?"

"About Magellan in St. Louis, and these morons here in Oklahoma City."

"I didn't know any of them."

"That may be true," Clint said, "but you know something you're not telling me."

"Clint, I swear—"

"Don't swear," Clint said. "It's just going to make it that much harder when I find out for sure later that you've been lying."

He picked his fork up again just as she put hers down.

"If you think I'm lying to you," she asked, "why are you agreeing to help me?"

"Because you're right," he said.

"About what?"

"I don't want you to get killed," he said. "I've killed enough people over the past few days."

"But you wouldn't be killing me," she said. "If what you say is true, somebody else would be killing me."

"I'd be letting you get killed if I let you go on alone," he responded. "Same thing."

"Then maybe that's it," she said. "After all these years you've suddenly got a conscience."

He didn't like her judging him that way.

"Conscience has nothing to do with it."

"No?" she asked. "What, then?"

He grinned at her and said, "Three thousand dollars."

TWENTY-FIVE

After lunch they left the hotel to go shopping. Rachel suggested they split up, but Clint rejected the idea.

"Who knows when somebody else is going to pop up to try to grab you?" he asked.

"So that means you'll come shopping for clothes with me?" she asked.

"What kind of clothes?" he asked.

"Well," she said, "as much as I'd like to get you into a dress shop, I'm going to need clothes I can travel on the trail with, right?"

"Right."

"So I need trousers," she said, "not dresses."

"And a sensible hat."

She made a face and said, "Sensible clothes are so boring."

"Then after we get you your clothes, we'll go and pick up some horses and a buckboard, and maybe a saddle."

"Are we buying, or renting?" she asked.

"I guess we'll have to find that out," he said. "I'm going to need a rifle, too, but I'll buy that myself."

"Why not?" she asked. "After all, I'm paying you three thousand dollars. Do you want it now?" she asked. "I'll have to go up to my room and get it."

"Do you expect me to believe you left all your money in your room?" he asked.

101

"Do you think I'd be walking around with that much money on me?" she demanded.

"Okay, it doesn't matter how much money you have on you," he said, "as long as you have some."

"Yes, I have some."

"Then let's go shopping."

Dutch Crater was angry.

He and his sons and Del Crockett, stood outside the train with the other passengers while the conductor explained to them what the problem was.

Dutch wasn't really listening to exactly what the mechanical problem was; he just wanted to know how long it was going to take to get it fixed.

"Goddamnit," he said, "we couldn't even get out of Missouri without this piece of crap breakin' down."

"Why don't we go into Joplin and get some horses, Pa?" Coy suggested.

"Because," Dutch said, "no matter how long it takes to fix this train, it's still gonna get us to Oklahoma City faster than horses will."

"Why are we goin' to Oklahoma City?" Sam asked. "I thought she was goin' to Texas."

Dutch rolled his eyes and looked at Luke.

"She is, Sam," Luke said, "but she's gonna have to stop in Oklahoma City first. We hope we can find out somethin' from Uncle Roy—or maybe he even grabbed her for us."

"If not," Del said, "we'll have to keep trailin' her into Texas."

"Luke," Dutch said, "go and ask that engineer what's goin' on."

"Pa, the conductor explained—"

"The conductor don't drive the damn train, does he?"

"No, Pa."

"Then go and talk to whoever does drive the damn train!"

"Yes, Pa."

"I'll come with you," Del said, and he and Luke proceeded to walk to the front of the train.

"Pa," Coy said, "I'm gonna go sit on that rock over there—"

"Sit wherever you want, Coy," Dutch said. "Just don't make me come lookin' for you, boy, when it's time to go, you hear?"

"I hear ya, Pa."

"Pa," Sam said, "can I go sit—"

"Jesus," Dutch said, "just go!"

TWENTY-SIX

Rachel was excited by the variety of stores that were available to her in Oklahoma City. By the time they had stopped at the fiftieth, Clint had had about enough.

"I thought you said you just needed some traveling clothes," he groused.

"But look at all these stores!" Rachel said. "How can I pass them up?"

"Okay," Clint said, "that does it." He ducked two women who were rushing into the boutique store just ahead of Rachel. "Give me some money and I'll go get the horses and the buckboard."

"How much do you want?"

"Five hundred."

They stepped aside to let a woman leave the store. Rachel turned her back, dug into her purse and came out with a handful of money, which she handed to him.

"That should do it."

"Just had it with you, huh?" he asked.

She smiled and said, "Just enough."

"But you kept some for what you need?"

"Oh, yeah."

"Okay," he said. "I'm going over to the nearest livery stable. Where are you going to be after this?"

"The next store," she said. "I'm just going to work my way down this street."

"All right," he said. "Don't leave this street. Do you have your gun with you?"

"Right here," she said, patting her thigh through her dress.

"We're going to have to get you something else to carry when you start wearing pants," he said. "When I go looking for a rifle, we'll get you something."

"Shopping for guns together," she said. "It sounds so romantic."

"I'm warning you, Rachel," he said. "There's nothing funny about this. Don't leave this street until I get back."

"Don't worry," she said. "From the looks of this fancy boutique, I probably won't even get out of here before you get back."

"That would suit me," he said.

"Go," she said. "Get us some good horses."

"You can ride, can't you?"

"I thought you were getting a buckboard."

"I thought we'd hook one horse to the buckboard and saddle the other one," he said. "We could switch off. You can ride, right? Western style?"

"Don't worry," she said, "I can ride. Just get the best horses you can find."

"I'll see you in a little while," he said. "Don't spend all of my money in there."

"Don't worry," she said. "The rest of your three thousand is safe."

He stopped short and turned back to her.

"This five hundred doesn't come out of my three thousand," he told her. "You're footing the bills for this expedition, remember?"

"Well," she said, "you can't blame a girl for trying."

Clint found a large livery stable which advertised the fact that they rented and sold horses, buggies and buckboards. He found the proprietor, a veteran horse handler named Rufus Wheeler, who took him out back to a corral.

"You lookin' to buy or rent?" the man asked, scratching his grizzly gray beard.

"I'm not sure," Clint said. "I'm going to be taking them to Texas."

"What part of Texas?"

"Heading for Austin."

Wheeler scratched his beard again. Clint didn't know if it itched, or if he just did that when he was thinking.

"I think yer gonna have ta buy," the man said. "I let you rent some animals and take them to Austin, I might never see 'em again—no offense intended."

"None taken,"

"Anythin' can happen between here and there."

"That's true. Okay, then. I'm looking to buy two horses, a buckboard and a saddle."

"Saddle, huh?" Scratch, scratch. "I think I got somethin' inside."

Clint went into the corral, examined most of the twenty or so animals that were in there and made his choice. He picked an eight-year-old bay mare to hook up to the buckboard because she was solidly built and looked to have a lot of miles left in her.

As a saddle mount he picked a dark gray four-year-old gelding that stood about fifteen hands and had some spirit to him. For the first time he lamented his decision to leave his Darley Arabian, Eclipse, behind in Epitaph. There was no way he could depend on another horse the way he could have depended on Eclipse.

"Now how about that buckboard?"

"Around the side," the liveryman said.

Clint followed him to where he had two buckboards and two buggies standing. Clint checked the axles on the buckboards, because the last thing they needed was to get stranded. He checked the wheels and didn't like the left rear one.

"I'll need this replaced."

The old man scratched his beard, then bent and examined the wheel himself before agreeing.

"Can you have it done by tomorrow?"

"You leavin' tomorrow?"

"I hope so," he said. He kept it to himself that it was up to the police. That might have kept the man from selling him the horses and buckboard.

"I think I can get it done," Wheeler said. "You want to see that saddle?"

"Show me."

He took Clint inside and showed him a saddle that had too much silver on it for his taste. The leather was good, though, and there wasn't much wear to it.

"Fella left this behind when he, uh, had to leave real quick."

"Leave?"

"He took a bullet," Wheeler explained. "Ended up six feet under. I got to keep the saddle against what he owed me." Wheeler reached into a stall and came out with a set of saddlebags. "Got these, too, which I'll toss in."

Clint took the saddlebags and examined them. They were older than the saddle, but serviceable.

"Okay," Clint said, "let's talk price for everything."

"Wanna do it over a drink?" Wheeler asked. "I got a bottle inside."

"Sounds good," Clint said, "as long as the drink is included."

Rufus Wheeler cackled and said, "I can already see you're a born haggler!"

TWENTY-SEVEN

When Clint got back to the boutique where he'd left Rachel, she wasn't there. He went up to the desk clerk to ask about her, and the woman eyed him with obvious fear and suspicion, but told him that Rachel had left an hour ago.

He left the store and started down the street to the next likely one . . .

After Clint left to go buy the horses, Rachel had come out of the boutique and made her way back to the hotel. She didn't go into the building, though, but into the stables where—unnoticed—she went to the stall that was housing the coffin. Clint had rented the stall as if for a horse. Rachel approached the coffin, knelt next to it, did something to a couple of the nails and lifted the lid open . . .

Clint tried three more stores. Just when he was about to give up, he found her in a hat shop, trying on hats that would definitely not help her on their trip.

"There you are," he said, coming up behind her as she tried on something purple with feathers.

She eyed him in the mirror and said, "Are you done?"

"As far as transportation is concerned, yeah. You're not really going to buy that hat, are you?"

"No," she said. "Don't worry. I bought the right kind.

They're holding it at the counter for me." She took off the feathered thing, set it aside and turned to face him.

"What's next?" she asked.

"Guns."

"Let me pay for my hat."

Not only were they holding the hat at the counter for her, but several other packages that were wrapped in brown paper, from other stores. She wore her new hat, a cream-colored, wide-brimmed Stetson. As they left, Rachel tried to get Clint to carry some of the packages, but he declined.

"I don't know how you're going to take them with us," he said, "but you bought them, so you have to carry them. After everything that's happened, I need my hands free."

"I guess I can't complain about you not being a gentleman," she said. "After all, you have saved my life a couple of times."

"You saved mine earlier today."

"Did I?" she asked. "I think you could have handled that man. I just wanted to do my part and show you I'm not totally helpless."

"Well," he said, "he could have gotten a lucky shot off at me, so I appreciate the fact that you're not helpless."

They walked along, looking for a gun shop, or a gunsmith, and Clint said, "You didn't stay in that store for long. What was it called?"

"A boutique," she said. "They have clothes and hats from places like Paris, France."

"Sounded to me like you left right away."

"I did," she said. "I guess fashions from Paris are not for me."

After a few more blocks, Rachel asked, "Where did you think I'd gone?"

"I didn't know."

She shifted her packages in her arms and nudged him with a shoulder.

"You thought I went off somewhere to do . . . what? Meet some mysterious lover?"

"I was just . . ." He let it trail off.

"What? Worried?" she asked, seductively. "Were you worried about me, Mr. Adams?"

"I'm committed to this venture, Rachel," he said. "If you get killed before we ever start, then I've wasted time, not to mention money."

"My money," she reminded him. "Don't forget."

"I won't."

"Speaking of which, any of that five hundred left?"

"Plenty."

"Good," she said. "You can use it for the guns, and if there's any left, you can buy me supper."

They finally came across a gun shop, and when they got inside, Rachel started to get sort of excited. She put her packages down on the glass counter and started to ooh and ahh over the guns inside.

Clint knew what he wanted, and quickly picked out a Winchester. After that they had to buy Rachel a handgun.

"And a rifle," she said.

"Can you shoot a rifle?" he asked.

"I can shoot anything."

"I think I'll have you prove that to me once we get outside the city limits."

He got a second Winchester for her, and then settled on a used handgun, a .32-caliber Colt Paterson.

"Perfect gun for the lady," the clerk said. "Not too big, not too small."

"Got a holster for it?" Clint asked.

"I got the perfect holster for it," the man said. "It's a used gun, and this is the holster I got it with."

He brought it out from beneath the counter and handed it to Rachel, who wanted to try it on, but couldn't with her dress on.

"Do you have a back room?" she asked. "I'd like to change."

"Sure," he said. "Go into the storeroom."

She grabbed some of her packages and took them into the back room with her, along with the new gun and holster.

"She's very excited," the clerk said.

"She's excitable."

"Are you two going on a trip?"

"Yes," Clint said, "a long one."

"You're going to need extra shells."

Clint looked at the man, feeling foolish that he had to be reminded.

"Yes, we are."

TWENTY-EIGHT

By the time Rachel came back out, Clint had bought boxes of shells for the rifles, her handgun and his own gun. At one point he saw the clerk's eye fall upon his holstered gun, and the man's eyes widened.

Rachel came out, dressed for the trail in a shirt, trousers and boots, and around her hips was the holstered Colt. Under her arm she had only one more brown paper package.

"You can throw out all of the things I left in the back," she told the man.

"Fine."

"Where's the derringer?" Clint asked.

"For now, it's here," she said, and brought it out from behind her belt.

"That's as good a place as any," he told her, and she tucked it away again. He turned to the clerk, said, "Let's settle up" and started counting money out onto the counter.

"Save enough to eat with," she said.

"There's plenty."

The clerk collected the money, still eyeing Clint with caution.

"Thanks for your help," Clint said to him.

"Yes, thank you," Rachel said.

"Anytime."

113

They left the store, and once outside, Rachel asked, "What did you do to him while I was changing?"

"Nothing," he said. "He saw my gun."

"And?"

"He recognized it."

She looked down at the gun on his hip.

"Is it that famous?"

"Apparently."

"Because of these?" She touched the indented grips in the handle.

"Yes."

"Your fingers fit right into there?"

"They do."

"That's amazing."

"Do you want to eat at the hotel again?"

"No," she said, "I want to eat where my clothes will help us blend in."

"A café, then," he said. "I think we passed one a couple of blocks back."

"Let's go, then," she said. "I'm starving."

They walked back three blocks and discovered Clint was right. There was a small café doing a brisk business. Inside they managed to find an empty table and order some dinner without attracting undue attention. The diners seemed to be interested only in what was going on at their own tables, and the level of conversation was a constant hum.

Clint was uncomfortable because they ended up at a table in the center of the room. His back itched, as if it had a bull's-eye on it, but he managed to get through his meal of beef stew and pie.

"You always order chicken," he said to Rachel.

"I like chicken."

"There's not going to be any chicken on the trail," he said.

"I'll do without, then," she said. "For now I'll just keep having chicken while I can get it."

He didn't argue with her, but he wondered how she would hold up to the hardships of the trip they were about to embark on.

And more than that, he wondered how the body of her

husband was going to hold up. He didn't know a lot about embalming and wondered just how long it would be before the body began to smell. If that happened, maybe he'd be able to bury her husband wherever they happened to be in Texas.

He didn't relish traveling all over South Texas with a rotting corpse attracting the buzzards.

TWENTY-NINE

When Clint and Rachel returned to the Continental Hotel, they found Sheriff Brody waiting for them in the lobby.

"Stopped in to see how you folks were doin'," he said.

"Checking up on us, Sheriff?"

"Clint," Rachel said, "I think the sheriff is just showing concern, aren't you, Sheriff?" She turned her seductive gaze on the lawman, who wilted noticeably beneath it.

"Yes, ma'am," he said, "and may I say you look very different, but just as pretty as this mornin'."

"Why, thank you, Sheriff."

"Have you got some news for us?"

"Well, I heard that you're gonna get a visit from the sergeant," Brody said. "He wanted to arrest you, like he told you, but his betters have told him to let you leave town."

"That's good news," Rachel said.

"They feel the same way I feel, Clint," Brody said. "The quicker you get out of town, the better."

"Why does everybody say that?" Rachel said. "None of the men he's killed have been his faul—"

"Never mind, Rachel," Clint said. "We want to leave town tomorrow, anyway. As long as they're going to let us leave, I don't really care what the reason is."

"Have you outfitted for your trip?" Brody asked.

"Just about," Clint said. "I bought a buckboard, and as long

117

as they can replace one of the wheels by tomorrow, I think we can be on our way. We'll just need to pick up some foodstuffs in the morning."

"Well, you can do that right down the street."

"Thanks for the tip, Sheriff," Clint said.

"Ma'am," Brody said, "I hope you are able to get your husband's coffin where you want it to be."

"Thank you, Sheriff," she said. "Clint, I'm going to go to my room now. I'll see you in the morning."

Both men watched her walk to the stairs and ascend to the second floor of the hotel.

"She's a handsome woman," Brody said. "A man could do worse."

"I suppose."

Brody looked at Clint.

"Are you married, Clint?"

"No."

"Ever been?"

"No."

"I was," Brody said, "for seven years before she died. Best seven years of my life. Can't wait to meet the right woman and get married again."

"Well," Clint said, "she may be coming back this way when she's done what she set out to do."

"You wouldn't mind?"

"Sheriff," Clint said, "I just work for the woman."

"You're takin' money to help her?"

"Of course," Clint said. "Why else would I be doing it?"

"I thought . . . Well, I thought wrong, I guess," Brody said. "I'd better be goin'."

"Thanks for the information."

"I figure the sergeant will make you wait until mornin' before he stops in."

"We'll be ready for him."

"Then with luck," Brody said, "I won't be seein' you again."

"Then let's hope for that luck."

Brody nodded and left the lobby of the hotel. Clint thought the lawman probably didn't have a high opinion of him, but he didn't care one way or the other.

Instead of going to his own room, he headed for the hotel bar to have one beer, his daily limit. There was a time he didn't know when to stop drinking, but that time was getting farther and farther behind him. It had been some time since he'd exceeded that one-beer-a-day allowance, and he didn't see any reason why tonight would be any different.

Rachel went to her room, removed the gunbelt and hung it on the bedpost. She took the gun from the holster, palmed it, checked to make sure it was loaded, then returned it. She couldn't wait for them to get past the city limits so she could prove to Clint that she could shoot. She thought he'd be surprised.

She thought about sneaking down to the coffin, but decided against it. She might run into Clint in the lobby. Instead, she decided to make herself comfortable, as this would be her last night in a real bed for quite a while.

THIRTY

Clint had just returned to his room when there was a soft knock on his door. He opened it and found Rachel standing in the hall, wearing a tightly belted robe. The cinched-in belt showed off her small waistline and large breasts. Somehow, when she was dressed, she didn't look as buxom as she did now.

"Can't sleep," she said. "I've been waitin' for you to come back. Can I come in?"

"Sure."

She slid past him to enter the room, and he caught her fresh, clean scent. He closed the door and turned to face her.

"Who are we kiddin'?" she said then. "We both know why I'm here."

With that, she undid the belt and let the robe fall to the floor. Beneath she was gloriously naked.

"Rachel—" he said, but his mouth was dry and he couldn't finish.

She smiled and said, "That's the reaction I was hoping for."

She came close enough for him to feel the heat from her body.

"Do you wear that gun to bed?" she asked.

"No."

She undid the buckle on his gunbelt, then backed away, letting it dangle from his hand.

"Put it on the bedpost," he said.

She obeyed, turning and walking to the bedpost, giving him a wonderful view of her undulating butt. Then she turned and looked at him over her bare right shoulder. Her long hair looked impossibly black against her pale skin.

"Are you going to join me on the bed?"

"Not with all these clothes on, I'm not."

He had the presence of mind to turn and lock the door as she climbed into bed. He removed his clothes while she watched, and he swore her gaze got hotter and hotter until he was naked.

"Um," she said, looking down at his thickening penis, "come here."

He walked to the bed and she greeted him on her knees. He put his hands on her shoulders, then slid his palms down her breasts until he was cupping them, holding the swollen under-sides in his hands, hefting their weight.

"They're too big," she said.

"They're just right."

"They'll sag when I get older."

"That's not going to happen in the next hour," he told her.

Her nipples were dark brown and distended. He lifted her breasts and bent to take one nipple, then the other, into his mouth. She moaned deep in her throat, almost a purr. Clint got down on his knees and continued to kiss her, moving his mouth over her ribs and belly, reaching behind her to cup her buttocks in his hands. When he reached the moist tangle of hair between her legs, he breathed in the heady scent of her. When he delved into the wet forest with his tongue, she gasped and fell onto her back on the bed, spreading her legs for him.

"Oh God," she said, as he stayed with her, keeping his face and his mouth pressed to her, sliding his hands beneath her now, to lift her to his mouth.

"God," she gasped, reaching for his head. "What are you doin' . . . ?

He didn't answer, but continued to lick her. If she had never had this done to her before by a man, she was in for a surprise. He abandoned her for a moment so he could kiss and nibble at the tender flesh of her inner thighs, but then went right back to work on her dripping pussy.

She placed her hands flat on the bed and took a handful of the sheet in each. She began to cry out and dig her heels into the bed, lifting her butt on her own so that he no longer had to lift her. She pressed her crotch into his face, gasping and moaning with each thrust of his tongue, and when he slid first one finger of his right hand into her inferno, and then another, she went off like fireworks at the Fourth of July. She began to beat on the bed with both her hands and her heels as a quake went through her body.

Without waiting for the tremors to stop, he got on the bed with her, mounted her and pushed his rigid cock deeply into her. She was so wet that he slid in easily, to the hilt, causing her breath to catch in her throat. He began pounding her, and she reached for him, wrapping her arms and her legs around him, begging him for more. At least, he thought she was begging for more. She was babbling so quickly that he could only catch a word here or there, but mostly he thought he heard, ". . . don't . . ." and ". . . stop . . . ," and from the way she was holding him to her, he knew she wasn't asking him to stop— and even if she was, there was no way he could have. He was caught in the fever of it, plunging in and out of her, aware that she was spasming again and again beneath him, but really seeking his own pleasure now.

He could feel his own release welling up inside of him, as if it were building up through his legs and into his groin. He felt his penis swell more and more inside of her, surrounded by the intense molten heat of her, and then he was exploding, his own shouts drowning hers out . . .

Later Rachel slid down between his legs and slowly stroked him until he was hard again.

"You're beautiful," she said, sliding her hand up and down the length of him.

"Rachel—" he said, thinking *he* should be telling *her* that, but suddenly she was on him with her mouth, licking him, wetting him, and then sucking him, and it was very hard to think of anything else . . .

THIRTY-ONE

While Clint was enjoying a breakfast of steak and eggs the next morning, he saw Sergeant Dan Tanner enter the dining room. The policeman looked around, located Clint and walked over to the table.

"Adams."

"Good morning, Sergeant," Clint said. "Coffee?"

Tanner hesitated, then said, "Sure, why not?"

He pulled out a chair and sat down. A waiter immediately appeared and filled a cup with coffee.

"Anything else, sir?" he asked.

"No," Tanner said. "Just go away."

"Sir."

"You insulted my waiter," Clint said. "I'm probably not going to get good service anymore."

"What does it matter?" Tanner asked. "You'll be leaving today anyway."

"Is that what you came here to tell me?" Clint asked.

"That's right. My superiors have told me to give you the okay to leave town."

"I appreciate that, Sergeant."

"Don't thank me," Tanner said. "I wanted to keep you around a little longer, until I found more witnesses. They decided it would make more sense to get you out of town as soon as possible."

"Was it their idea for you to come and tell me, then?"

"No, that was my idea," Tanner said. "I wanted to tell you that I'm not impressed with you."

"Well, Sergeant," Clint replied, "I'm not much impressed with you, either."

"That's fine," Tanner said. He pushed away the cup of coffee, which he hadn't touched, and stood up. "I hope you're prepared to leave today."

"We're all set," Clint said, even though he wasn't sure the wheel had been replaced yet.

"Good," Tanner said. "Do us all a favor and don't come back here . . . ever."

"Don't worry," Clint said. "To tell you the truth, the food here hasn't been very good."

"Do you think it's funny that you came here and killed three men?" the policeman asked.

"Not at all," Clint said. "I think it's sad that three men chose a course of action that caused them to die."

"They didn't just die," Tanner said. "You killed them. Your time is done, Adams. There's no room for your kind anymore."

"My kind?" Clint asked.

"The fast gun," Tanner said, "the shootist, whatever you want to call yourself."

"Sergeant," Clint said, "I don't think you know what you're talking about."

"Don't I?"

"I think it'd be best if we didn't talk to each other anymore."

By this time they had attracted some attention in the dining room, including that of Rachel, who had just entered.

Tanner swept back the flap of his coat to reveal the gun he carried in a shoulder rig.

"You wanna try me, gunman?"

Clint pushed his chair back but did not get up.

"Tanner," Clint said, "you'd be dead before you could get your gun out of that fancy rig, and what would be the point? Your bosses would still let me leave, because you pushed this, and there are witnesses. You see, I kill when I have no choice. Now it's up to you. Are you going to give me a choice?"

Tanner glared at Clint, who could see the fire dying in the man's eyes as he realized Clint was right. The policeman released his jacket, turned and stormed out of the room, brushing past Rachel.

"What was that all about?" Rachel asked, when she reached the table.

"The sergeant was a little upset." Clint pulled his chair close to the table as Rachel sat down.

"Why didn't you wake me?" she asked. Sometime during the night she had returned to her own room so they could both get some sleep.

"I thought you'd be too exhausted."

"Me?" She grinned. "You're the one who should be exhausted."

"Okay," he said, "let's agree we were both exhausted. I'll get the waiter over here to get you some breakfast, and then we better be on our way. That fool might change his mind and come back and force me to do it after all."

THIRTY-TWO

When they got to the livery, their horses and buckboard were all ready. The rear wheel had been replaced, but Clint took the time to get down and check the axles again, to be sure that another buckboard had not been substituted.

"You're a suspicious man, Mr. Adams," Rufus Wheeler said. "I like you."

"Just playing it safe, Rufus," Clint said.

"I didn't know if you wanted that other horse saddled or not, so I just put the bridle on him and tied him to the back of the wagon."

"That's good for now, Rufus," Clint said. "I'll saddle him when we got outside of town."

Clint walked around and climbed up onto the buckboard seat alongside Rachel.

"Good luck on your trip," Wheeler bade them.

"Thank you," Rachel said, but Clint simply snapped the reins at the horse and drove away.

They drove to the Continental Hotel so that Clint could check them out and then pick up the coffin. He paid the livery man a few extra dollars to help him load the box on the back of the buckboard.

Rachel reached around from her position on the seat and placed her hand on the top of the coffin.

"We're on our way again, Ethan," she said.

"Are you going to do that the whole way?" he asked.

"Do what?"

"Talk to a dead man?"

"You don't think the dead can hear us?"

"The dead are dead, Rachel," he said. "I've killed enough men to know that they can't hear us anymore."

He secured the back of the buckboard, then came around to climb up next to her. The next stop was a mercantile, for traveling supplies.

A half an hour later they had supplies in the back of the buckboard, on both sides of the coffin: coffee, flour, bacon, sugar, peaches and more. Clint preferred to travel light, but since they had the buckboard he decided to load up. It would probably be safer for them if they didn't have to stop in too many towns along the way. He'd also purchased blankets, ponchos and bedrolls.

"Is that all?" Rachel asked, when he climbed up next to her.

"It should be enough."

"Looks like enough for months on the trail."

"It's not," he said. "With any luck, though, it should take us to Austin."

"No stops along the way?" she asked.

"Not in towns," he said. "If anybody else wants to take a shot at you or me, they're going to have to track us and do it on the trail."

She waited for him to get the buckboard moving, and when he didn't she said, "What are we waiting for?"

He turned to face her.

"Is there anything you want to tell me before we start?"

"Like what?"

"Just anything you think I should know."

"No, Clint," she said, "I don't have anything to tell you." She put her hand on his arm. "Except that I think you're a wonderful man."

"You still have to pay me, you know," he said, "even though we slept together."

Now she slapped his arm and said, "I know that."

"Okay," he said. "Then I guess we'd better get going."

"Finally," she said. "Can I drive?"

"Do you know how to drive a rig?"

"Can I drive, can I shoot, can I ride?" she said. "I'm going to have to prove it all to you, aren't I?"

He handed the reins to her and said, "You might as well start with this."

THIRTY-THREE

Sergeant Dan Tanner watched as Clint Adams and Rachel Chandler drove away from the Continental Hotel in their rented buckboard. He was still stinging from Clint making him back down in the dining room. He wished he'd gone for his gun, because even being dead would be better than the way he was feeling right now.

When Tanner got back to police headquarters, he found a message at his desk telling him his boss, Captain Jennings, wanted to see him. He walked to the man's office and knocked on the door.

"Come!"

Tanner entered, closed the door and waited.

"What happened with Adams?" Captain Dale Jennings asked.

"He's gone," Tanner said. "He and the woman just left."

"How are they traveling?"

"They rented a buckboard."

"How well stocked?"

"Extremely well."

Jennings sat back in his chair. He was fifty-five years old, and had the midsection of a man who'd been sitting behind a desk for a long time. His hope was that, within the next two years, he would be appointed chief of police. It was Jennings who had brought Tanner from the East to be his protégé.

"They don't intend to stop anywhere along the way," he said. "Not if they've outfitted that well."

"Apparently not."

"All right," Jennings said. "Tomorrow morning I want you to take ten men and go after them."

"What?"

"I want you to arrest Clint Adams and bring him back."

"Arrest him . . . for what?"

"Murder."

Tanner was confused.

"I don't understand," he said. "We had him here and could have arrested him. Is this for the murder of . . . who?"

"Keenan and Bobo Miller, and Roy Frump."

"But . . . Clint didn't kill Frump," Tanner said. "The woman did."

"Then bring her back, too," Jennings said, "under arrest."

"But . . . why?"

Jennings stood up, went to the door to make sure it was closed, then stepped up close to Tanner, put his lips almost to the younger man's ears.

"Do you know what it would mean for me—for us—to put Clint Adams, the Gunsmith, behind bars for murder? Publicity, lots of publicity."

Jennings walked around to stand in front of Tanner.

"I can ride publicity like that right into the chief of police's job, Dan," Jennings said, "and beyond."

"Beyond?"

"The mayor's mansion."

"Mayor?"

Jennings shrugged and asked, "Why not?"

"And . . . what would it mean to me?" Tanner asked.

"A promotion," Jennings said, "right from sergeant to captain."

"And all this just for arresting Clint Adams?"

"Arresting him," Jennings said, "and killing him when he tries to escape."

"Kill—who's going to kill him?"

"You are."

Tanner frowned. "When? Where?"

"Out there," Jennings said, "somewhere. Between where

you finally catch him, and here. Somewhere along the way, put a bullet in him."

"But . . . what about the other men?"

"Pick them carefully," Jennings said. "Find two or three who want promotions. Figure it out, Dan. This can help all of us."

Tanner only had to give it a moment's thought. The sting from backing down from Clint that morning was still fresh.

"Captain," he said, "I think I know four men who will come with me, and do as they're told. I don't need ten."

"Remember, Sergeant," Jennings said, "this man has a reputation."

"Reputation or not, he's only one man," Tanner said, "and he's getting on in years."

"Hm, yes," Jennings said. "About my age, isn't he?"

Tanner didn't know what to say to that, so he remained silent while the captain walked around and seated himself behind his desk again.

"All right, Sergeant," Jennings said, "this is in your hands. Be careful about who you talk to."

"Yes, sir."

"Let me know when you have your men picked and who they are. You'll be leaving at first light."

"Yes, sir," Tanner said. "I'll take care of it."

Tanner turned and left the captain's office. He stopped just outside the door and took a deep, satisfying breath. He was going to have his chance with Clint Adams after all.

Captain Dale Jennings stared at the closed door of his office after Tanner left. He hoped he wasn't making a mistake trusting the young sergeant.

THIRTY-FOUR

"Rein it in," Clint said.

"Why?"

"Do it."

Rachel reined the horse in and halted their progress. Clint dropped down to the ground.

"What's going on?" she asked.

"We're outside the city limits," he said. "Time for you to show me your shooting skills."

"You mean you're satisfied with my ability to drive a buckboard?" she asked.

"Yes, I am," he said. "Next I want to see you shoot. I need to know if I can depend on you in a firefight."

"I didn't prove that yesterday?"

"You proved you could press the barrel of a gun against a man's head and pull the trigger," he said. "That was admirable. Now I need to know if you can hit what you shoot at from a greater distance."

Rachel tied the reins to the handbrake and dropped down to the ground. She reached into the back of the buckboard, came out with her holster and strapped it on. Next she retrieved her Winchester from the same place. Finally, she walked around to the back of the buckboard, where Clint was standing.

"What do I shoot first?"

"That rock," he said, pointing. "See it? In the clearing, about the size of a can of peaches."

"I see it," she said. "It's not very far away. About thirty feet?"

"More like forty," he said. "Far enough for me."

"Rifle or handgun first?"

"Rifle."

She pressed the butt of the rifle to her shoulder, sighted down the barrel and fired. The rock in question skipped and came to a stop about three feet farther away.

"Do it again."

"Why?"

"So I know it wasn't a fluke."

She shouldered the rifle again and fired. This time the rock skipped sideways, as instead of hitting it flush the bullet struck it on one side. A near miss, if one were looking for something to complain about.

"Not bad," he said. "Now the pistol."

She put the Winchester into the back of the buckboard and hefted the gunbelt on her hips.

"I'm not a fast draw," she said.

"Neither am I," he said. "I'm more concerned that you can hit what you aim at."

"The same target?"

"Yes."

She spread her legs, checked to be sure the weapon wouldn't stick in the holster, then drew it and fired. The bullet kicked up dirt in front of the rock, missing by about a foot. She adjusted, fired again and missed six inches to the left.

"Damn."

"That's enough."

"I can hit it."

"That's okay," he said. "You came close enough. If there was a man there, you would have hit him."

"But I can hit it," she said again.

"All right," he said. "Go ahead."

She fired again, then a fourth time, before the rock finally skipped away.

"Ha!"

As she started to holster the weapon, Clint said, "Now re-load."

"Now?"

"Don't ever holster your weapon without reloading," he said. "The next time you draw it, you've got to know that you're fully loaded."

She ejected the spent shells and then reloaded the gun before holstering it again.

"We'll have to work on your speed."

"Drawing?"

"Reloading," he said.

"Okay," she said. "Now you."

"What?"

"I get to see you shoot," she said. "I've got to know I can count on you, too, don't I?"

He was going to protest, but decided to simply do as she asked, so he drew and fired once, twice and again, and the rock jumped and skidded three separate times. He fired a fourth time and the rock leaped into the air, and then he fired a fifth time and hit it before it came back to ground.

Quickly, he ejected the spent shells, reloaded and holstered his gun. When he looked at Rachel, she was just staring at him with her mouth hanging open.

"Satisfied?"

"I—I've never seen anything like that," she said. "It was . . . fast."

"It's more important to be accurate."

"I see," she said. "Well . . . now do you want to see me ride?"

The saddle was in the back of the buckboard, and he didn't want to put it to use until he made some modifications.

"No," he said. "We'll leave that for tomorrow. Let's get moving again."

"Who's driving?"

"You are."

"Then let's go," she said. "We still have plenty of daylight."

THIRTY-FIVE

They traveled until dusk, and then Clint decided to camp early.

"It's the first day out," he said. "I don't want to push you too hard."

"I'm fine," she said.

"Well then, I don't want to push the horses too hard. I'm going to go and collect some wood for a fire."

"What do I do?"

"Can you unhitch the horse?"

"I think I can manage it."

"Good," he said. "When I get back with the wood, you can start cooking while I bed the horses down."

"I'll do my part, Clint," she said. "Don't worry about that."

"If I didn't think you'd do your part, Rachel, I wouldn't be here," he said.

He gathered some wood, brought it back and built a fire near the buckboard. When that was done, she collected what she needed from out of the buckboard, and he went and took care of the horses. By the time he got back, there was coffee, and bacon and beans were cooking in a frying pan.

"So, you can cook," he said, sitting down next to her.

"Of course I can cook," she said. "What kind of a pampered, helpless woman did you think I was?"

"I never thought that."

"What did you think?"

"When?"

"That first day you saw me on the dock in St. Louis, sitting on the coffin?"

"I thought, 'Now there's a crazy woman.' "

She laughed with her head tossed back so he could see her pale throat.

"At least you're honest."

She handed him a plate and they settled down to eat.

After the meal was over, he left her to clean up while he went and fetched the saddle from the buckboard. He put it on the ground near the fire, took out a knife and started working on it.

"What are you doing to that poor saddle?" she asked. "It looks like you're gouging out chunks of it."

"The idiot who owned it had all this silver on it," he said.

"Probably because it was pretty that way," she said. "Now look what you've done to it."

"Well, it may have been pretty, but it wasn't very practical. The sun would reflect off all this silver and somebody would be able to see us from miles away."

"Oh," she said, "I see . . . And there is someone looking for us, isn't there?"

"For you, I suppose," he said.

"Me? It's you everybody's trying to kill."

"No, Rachel," he said, without looking up from the saddle. "I think we both know it's you, but only one of us knows why, and that person isn't talking."

When she didn't respond, he looked at her, and while she stared down at her hands in her lap, he added, "At least, not yet."

"You're going to have to take a watch," he said, later, when they were getting ready to turn in. "Either the first four hours, or the last. I won't last very long if I'm on watch all night and riding all day."

"So we won't be sleeping together?" she asked, playfully.

"Not while we're on the trail, Rachel," he said.

"Guess I should have gotten a little more in the hotel, then."

"This is serious, Rachel," he said, scolding her—although, he wouldn't have minded a little more, too.

"All right. I think I'd prefer the first watch."

"That's fine," he said. "A few things."

"Yes?"

"Don't look directly into the fire," he explained. "It'll destroy your night vision."

"All right."

"And listen to the horses. They'll give you fair warning if someone is coming—especially an animal, like a wolf, or a big cat."

"Or a man?"

"Probably that, too."

"Okay," she said, "I've got it."

"Keep your gun on," he said, rolling himself up in his bedroll. "You can take it off when you go to bed, if you like."

"You're not taking yours off," she noticed.

"After years of sleeping on the trail, I wouldn't be able to fall asleep if I took it off."

"Anything else?"

"Yes," he said, putting his head down on his saddle. "Make sure there's a fresh pot of coffee when you wake me."

"Yes, sir."

For the first hour she was on watch, Rachel was tempted to look into the fire. She knew it was because Clint had told her not to. She was also tempted to go and take a look at the coffin, but there was really no need. It had been with them all day, and she could see it from where she was. She looked over at Clint, who seemed to be sleeping soundly, but there was no way to be sure.

No, she'd leave the coffin alone at night. Besides, what was inside wasn't going anywhere.

THIRTY-SIX

As the first ribbons of sunlight came down from above, Clint turned and looked at the sleeping form of Rachel Chandler. During the night he'd been tempted to try to get a look inside the coffin, but it had been too dark, and it would have made too much noise. Also, he didn't like the idea that he was exhibiting some semblance of curiosity. It was not an emotion he had ever struggled with before, and he wasn't used to it.

He did, at one point during the night, walk up to the buckboard, lean in and take a deep breath. No odor. That was what was making him curious, he realized. There was just no odor.

He prepared a fresh pot of coffee, then went over and nudged Rachel awake with his hand on her shoulder. If she'd been a man, he would have used the toe of his boot.

"Time to get up."

He was impressed with the fact that she rolled right out and got to her feet. He was also impressed that the first thing she did was set about making breakfast, and not worrying about how she looked—although she looked pretty damn good to him.

"You're wondering what I did before I got married, aren't you?" she asked.

"How did you know that?"

"I could feel you staring at me when I was asleep," she

said, "and I can feel your eyes boring into the back of my head now."

"So," he said.

"So what?" She dropped a slab of bacon into the frying pan.

"So . . . what *did* you do before you got married?"

She turned and looked at him over her shoulder. He saw little lines in her face that hadn't been there before—or maybe he hadn't noticed them. Whatever the case, they made her more attractive.

"I don't think we know each other well enough yet for me to talk about that, Clint."

"Fair enough, Rachel."

She finished making breakfast and handed him a plate, then poured him another cup of coffee.

"Did you hear anything during the night?" he asked her.

"No," she said. "If I had, I would have woke you up."

"Did you ever think you might have heard something?" He held up his hand, his thumb and forefinger about an inch apart. "Ever that close to waking me up?"

She studied him for a moment, then said, "Yes, I was."

"Why didn't you?"

"I decided it was my imagination."

"For the rest of this trip," he said, "whenever you're that far from waking me, do it."

"What if it is my imagination?"

"I'm more concerned with the time that it isn't your imagination, Rachel."

"I understand," she said. "I'm sorry."

"Don't be sorry," he said. "I just don't want anybody creeping up on us in the middle of the night."

After breakfast he said, "I'm going to saddle the other horse while you clean up. I'll want to ride a bit today."

"Will I be able to?" she asked. "I still have something to prove to you."

"No," he said, "you don't . . . but yes, you'll have a chance to ride."

She smiled and said, "Good."

Clint saddled the mount, pulling the cinch tight. Rachel had been right the day before when she said it now looked as if something had gouged it out in places, but he was satisfied with it now that all the silver had been removed.

With that done, he took the other horse to the buckboard and hitched it up. By that time Rachel had everything cleaned up and stowed away in back of the buckboard. At one point he noticed her put her hand on the coffin, leave it there a moment, then turn away and finish breaking camp. She doused the campfire without being told to, then got herself ready to go. The last thing she did was strap on her gun.

"You ready?" he asked.

"Ready."

"Then let's mount up."

Sergeant Dan Tanner studied the four men he had chosen to go with him after Clint Adams. They were all young, all ambitious and all ready to do what they had to do. They were dressed in trail clothes, not their uniforms, but each was wearing his badge on his chest.

Tanner had spoken to each of them separately the night before, told them that their job was to bring Clint Adams back to Oklahoma City—not necessarily alive. None of them questioned that statement, and all seemed to understand it.

Now they were all mounted and outfitted and ready to go.

"Before we leave," he called out, "does anyone have any questions about what we have to do?"

The men exchanged glances, but nobody spoke up.

"Anyone have any doubts?" he asked. "Anybody want to pull out, stay behind?"

They exchanged glances again, and then a man named Dave Cole said, "No, sir. We're all ready to do what has to be done."

"Excellent," Tanner said. "Then let's move out. You take the point, Officer Cole."

"Yes, sir."

"Move out!"

THIRTY-SEVEN

Dutch Crater got off the train in Oklahoma City, followed by Luke and Del Crockett. He turned and waited, then asked, "Where are your brothers?"

"They, uh, got into a poker game in the baggage car."

"Well, go get 'em, Luke," Dutch said. "I'm gonna talk to the ticket clerk."

"Why?"

"Because your uncle was supposed to meet the train here and grab Rachel," Dutch said. "That means he would've had to go through Adams to do it. Chances are, that woulda happened right here, like in St. Louis with Magellan."

"You want me to come with you?" Luke asked.

"Go and get your brothers," Dutch said. "Del, you come with me."

"Okay, Dutch."

Luke headed down the train to the baggage car while Dutch and Del went into the station.

Luke heard the shouting even before he reached the car. When he got there, his brothers were standing with their guns out, and the baggage handlers were standing with their hands up.

"What happened, Coy?" Luke asked.

"These boys were cheatin'," Coy said.

"We wasn't cheatin'," one of them said. "This feller tried to fill an inside straight and didn't."

"I woulda," Coy said, "with an honest deal."

"We dealt honest," the other handler said to Luke. "These boys is just bad poker players."

"We ain't bad—" Sam started, but Luke cut him off.

"Shut up, Sam," Luke said. "The man is right. You boys are terrible poker players."

"Who's side you on, Luke?" Coy demanded.

"I'm on Pa's side, and he wants you and Sam now."

"We want our money—"

"Put your guns away."

"Luke," Sam said, "we lost a lot—"

"Put your guns away, boys!" Luke snapped. "Don't make me come up there."

Coy looked at Luke, tried to stare him down but couldn't. Finally, he holstered his gun, and then Sam did the same.

"Now come on down from there and let's go."

Coy and Sam dropped down from the car, both looking real unhappy as they stormed off.

"You boys best be careful who you play poker with," Luke said.

"We won, didn't we?" one of them asked.

"Maybe," Luke said, "but if I hadn't gotten here, you'd also be dead right now."

He turned and followed his brothers.

Dutch entered the station and strode to the desk.

"Can I help you, sir?" the ticket clerk asked.

"I need some information," Dutch said.

"Our schedule is right on the wa—"

"Not about that," Dutch said. "I'm lookin' for someone, a relative of mine. He was waiting here for a train to arrive, yesterday."

"Yesterday," the clerk said. "Wow, that's when we had all the excitement."

Dutch tightened his lips and said, "Yeah, that's what I want to hear about . . ."

•   •   •

Dutch and Del came out of the station and found Luke, Coy and Sam waiting.

"What happened to Uncle Roy?" Luke asked.

"He's dead."

"What?"

"Him and two friends who sound like the Miller brothers," Dutch said. "Sounds like they grabbed Rachel comin' off the train—her and the coffin. Then some fella stepped in and killed 'em."

"All three of them?"

"From what the clerk says, it sounds like Clint Adams killed Bobo and Keenan, and Rachel killed Roy."

"She killed Uncle Roy?" Luke asked.

"That's what it sounds like."

"So what do we do now?"

"We outfit and go after them," Dutch said. "They're headed for Austin."

"We hope," Luke said.

"No," Dutch said. "That's where they're headed."

"Are we at least stayin' in town overnight?" Coy asked. "After all, we never been to Oklahoma City—"

"You got any money left, Coy?" Luke asked.

"Well, no, but—"

"Then you wouldn't have much fun here, would you?"

"Pa—"

"Let's find someplace to get some horses," Dutch said.

"We gonna buy 'em, Pa?" Sam asked. "We gonna need some money. Me and Coy can—"

"No," Dutch said, "we're in too much of a hurry for that. This time, we'll just take what we need."

THIRTY-EIGHT

Clint felt good being in the saddle and on the trail again. He'd ridden from St. Louis to St. Charles and back again, but that didn't have the same feel as what he was doing now.

"You look happy," Rachel said to him at one point, as he was riding alongside her.

"What?"

"Riding," she said. "It seems to make you happy."

"Yeah, it does, but I wish I had my own horse underneath me."

They rode awhile more in silence. Then she asked, "You've never been married, Clint?"

"No."

"Ever come close?"

"No."

"Come on," she said. "There must have been a woman sometime, somewhere?"

"There have been lots of women," he said, "but none I wanted to settle down with, and none who would settle down with a man like me."

"And what, exactly, is a man like you?"

"Someone who could be dead any minute."

"Oh." After a few moments she asked, "Doesn't that bother you?"

"Doesn't what bother me?"

"That you could be killed at any minute?"

"I've lived my life that way for a long time," he explained. "It's too late to stop it now."

"What if you just stopped wearing a gun?"

"I'd be dead the same day I did that," he said. "Can you imagine what would have happened over the past couple of days if I wasn't wearing a gun? I'd have been dead five times over."

"That's true." Now she frowned. "Whatever made you decide to live this life, anyway?"

"I asked you a question once and you told me we didn't know each other well enough for you to answer it."

"Yeah, but—"

"That's how I feel about this one."

"I understand, but—"

"I'm going to scout up ahead," he said. "We've got to make sure this road is clean for the buckboard."

As he rode away, she thought how strange men were, that they would set their lives up early in such a way that, even later in life, they were still stuck with it.

Then again, hadn't she done the same thing by marrying Ethan Chandler in the first place? That had been an act that would impact the rest of her life, and she'd known it when she did it.

Maybe that's how it was with him, too.

They'd been lucky so far, in that they hadn't had to turn back at any time because the buckboard couldn't make it over the terrain. It was generally a rule of thumb for Clint that doubling back meant doubling your travel time, so he liked to avoid it is much as possible. To that end he'd scouted ahead several times already, making sure that the way was clear for the buckboard.

This time, however, maybe he scouted ahead to get away from Rachel and her questions. What good did it do a man *now* to wonder how life would have been had he made a different decision *then*? That kind of thinking just led to beating yourself up. And he'd long decided he was going to live to the end of his life alone, without a woman, so why bother to wonder about that, either?

And normally, he didn't. Those questions went unanswered because he usually didn't ask them of himself, so he didn't need someone else asking them either. Did he?

THIRTY-NINE

The main problem became clear to Sergeant Tanner right away. He didn't know how to track, and he hadn't asked any of the men if they knew how. He couldn't admit that, though. Luckily, when the subject of tracking came up, Dave Cole told Tanner he knew how.

"You have experience?" Tanner asked, pulling him aside so the others couldn't hear.

"Yes, sir," Cole said. "My pa taught me how to track. I mean, I ain't an expert or a bounty hunter or nothin', but I can track."

"What do you need?"

"I need to see where the trail starts."

"At their hotel."

They rode to the hotel, and immediately they knew this wasn't going to work.

"There's been too much traffic, here," Cole said. "We don't know which tracks are theirs."

"Damn it!"

"Do we know where they're goin'?" Cole asked.

"I think, when we first questioned them, they said they were heading for South Texas."

Cole shrugged.

"We might as well head south and see what kind of tracks

157

we come across. You said they had a coffin in the back of the buckboard?"

"Yes."

"And supplies," Cole surmised. "The tracks left by the wagon will probably be deep."

Tanner was afraid. They had to leave right away, so they wouldn't be more than a day behind. That meant they didn't have time to try to find out where Adams rented his horses and rig from. Tanner was going to have to follow Cole's advice.

"All right," he said. "We'll ride due south and see what happens."

He felt the eyes of the other men on him. Did they realize how stupid he had been? He needed them to follow him and obey him without question.

"We should be able to pick out their tracks once we get away from the city," Cole said. "A buckboard and a saddle horse. Sometimes the horse may be tied to the back of the wagon, and sometimes he might be riding alongside."

"So you'll be able to pick out their tracks?"

"We're only a day behind them," Cole said. "I think so."

"All right," Tanner said. "Just don't mention anything about this to the others. All they are to know is that you are our tracker."

"Yes, sir."

"All right, then," Tanner said, "Let's get on with it."

Dutch and his sons and Del Crockett walked around Oklahoma City looking for a likely place to get horses from. It had to be a place off of a main street, not in plain sight, because they were going to steal what they needed.

It took a couple of hours, and Dutch was getting agitated.

"Why don't we split up?" Del suggested. "We might find somethin' faster that way."

"Okay," Dutch said. "Good idea."

"Del and I can go—" Luke started, but Dutch cut him off right away.

"No," Dutch said, pointing at Coy and Sam. "If we let these idiots go off on their own, they'll just get into trouble. Del, you take Coy, and Luke, you take Sam." He looked around for a moment, then saw what he wanted. "You boys see that little saloon?"

"Yes, Pa," Luke said.

"All right, we'll meet there in an hour. Somebody better have something for us. We need horses and saddles. After we get them, we'll pick up some supplies and get out of town fast."

"Okay," Del said. "Then let's go."

"We gonna steal the supplies, too, Pa?" Coy asked.

"We'll see about that, Coy," Dutch said. "We'll see."

An hour later Dutch was waiting in that small saloon, nursing a beer. He hoped that Coy and Sam—even though they were with Luke and Del—wouldn't find a way to get in trouble. He was relieved when Luke and Sam came walking in and approached his table.

"Anything?" he asked.

"Pa," Luke said, "we found one possible place, a small livery stable with a corral behind it."

"Okay, let's see what Del comes up with," Dutch said. "Get yourselves a beer while we wait."

"Sure, Pa."

Luke and Sam went to the bar and returned with a mug of beer each. They sat down to wait with their father.

"It's gettin' late," Dutch said. "I want us to get goin' before dark, so unless Del found someplace better, you're gonna have to take us back to the place you found."

"No problem, Pa."

Dutch played with his half-filled beer mug, checking the door from time to time, until finally, the batwings opened and Del came in with Coy right behind him.

"We found a place," Del said.

FORTY

It took them the better part of three days to get within spitting distance of Dallas. It also took the three days for several things to become clear.

First, Clint had to admit that he was curious about the coffin. Embalmed or not, if there was a body in there it would have to be giving off a smell after three days in the Texas sun, and it wasn't. There was something in that coffin that somebody didn't want Rachel to have. There had to be.

Second, Rachel was not going to be as pleasant a traveling companion for the rest of the trip as she had been the first two days. During the course of the third day her mood began to change as she sweated completely through another shirt.

And third, he liked her. If he didn't, he would have dumped the coffin out of the back of the buckboard and smashed it open to find out what was inside. Maybe she was entitled to what was inside, and whoever was after her wasn't.

As they camped the third night, she was grumbling about the constant heat during the day.

"Is Texas always this hot?"

"Most of the time."

"Can't we go into Dallas tomorrow?" she asked. "Or Fort Worth? I could use a bath, and would like to wash my clothes."

"The whole point of outfitting this well was to avoid towns, Rachel," he reminded her.

"I know, but my clothes—"

"You can't keep changing your shirt just because you sweat through it," Clint said.

"But it smells," she said, "and sticks to me."

"What did you expect this trip to be like, Rachel?"

"Well, I thought I'd be making the whole trip by train," she said, "or at least a stagecoach."

"You think this heat would be easier to take on a stage?"

"At least it wouldn't be beating down on me all day."

"Okay," he said, "if you want, I'll take you into Dallas tomorrow. You can catch a train or a stage there to Austin."

"What about you?"

"I'll head my own way."

"But . . . why? I'll pay for your passage. It can't be because you're afraid to be shot at."

"Not afraid," he said. "Tired of it. And I'm tired of killing people. I think traveling the rest of the way like this will avoid that."

She stared across the fire at him and finally stopped complaining about her clothes.

"You're not doing this for the money, are you?"

"I'm not?"

"No."

"Why am I doing it, then?"

She studied him for a few minutes. "I'm going to have to think about that for a while. There's something going on inside your head, though."

"I think we'll probably find water tomorrow," he said. "You can have a swim, wash some of the sweat off, and even clean your shirts, if you want."

"Ah," she said, "changing the subject."

"How about some more coffee?" he asked, holding out his cup.

She poured him some, and then took some more for herself.

"Rachel?"

"What?"

"What's in the coffin?"

"Are you curious?"

"I am," he said, "I have to admit."

"And you don't think it's my husband?"

"I think a body—even an embalmed one—would have started to . . . uh . . ."

"Smell by now?"

"At least be a little ripe."

"I tell you what I'll do, then," she said. "I'll make you a deal."

"What kind of deal?"

"I'll open the coffin and let you have a look."

"Or?"

"Or I'll pay you five thousand dollars when we get to Austin, instead of three."

"Do you have five thousand dollars?"

"Not on me," she said, "but I will when I get to Austin."

"And does this offer include a trip into Dallas or Fort Worth tomorrow?"

"No," she said, "you're right about that. A swim in a water hole, or a stream, or whatever, will do nicely. And I'll try to stop complaining about the heat."

Clint studied her.

"Five thousand, huh?"

"That's right," she said. "Get me to Austin alive and well, with my coffin, for five thousand."

Clint looked over at the buckboard with the coffin on it. Even if she was right and he hadn't been doing this for the money, five thousand dollars would put the whole thing in perspective. For five thousand he could forget about what was in the coffin and just look at this as a job—his last job, for a while.

"What do you say?" Rachel asked. "Do we have a deal?"

He switched his gaze from the coffin to her. "We have a deal."

FORTY-ONE

Just outside of Oklahoma City that first day, Cole thought he'd picked up the trail. He dismounted to study the ground, then called for Tanner to do the same.

"Looks like two horses, one pulling a buckboard, one following," he said.

"That sounds perfect," Tanner said. "Let's follow it."

They both straightened up and walked back to their horses.

"Officer Cole has picked up the trail," Tanner told the others. "It shouldn't be long now."

However, by the time they camped at the end of the second day, Tanner wasn't so sure they were following the right trail.

"We should have caught up to them by now," he told Cole. "After all, they're hauling a coffin."

"Well," Cole said, "we're following a trail left by two horses and a buckboard, sir. Could that be a coincidence?"

"Look," Tanner said. He took a moment to look behind them, where they had left the other three riders. "I'll take the rest of the men and keep following this trail. You go off on your own and scout around a bit. See if you can pick up another trail. If you do, then come back and get us."

"Yes, sir."

"I'll just tell the rest that you're scouting ahead."

"How long should I keep looking, sir?"

"Take some supplies," Tanner said. "You can camp

overnight and catch up to us tomorrow, hopefully with some news."

"Okay," Cole said. "I can do that, sir."

"Good," Tanner said. "Then do it." Tanner had each man carry some supplies, so they wouldn't have to take a pack-horse along to slow them down. "Take just enough to get you through one night, and give the rest of your supplies to the others. We'll see you tomorrow."

In the morning when they broke camp, Tanner took the rest of the men and continued to follow the trail, while Cole veered off to scout the area for a similar trail.

Del and Coy took Dutch, Luke and Sam to a small livery sta-ble they found at the east end of town. It was getting late, the end of their first day in Oklahoma City, and Dutch didn't want to spend a second day there. He didn't care if they had to leave after dark; they were not going to waste any part of a second day.

The area around the stable was pretty deserted, which made it a desirable target, but it also looked kind of run-down.

"Did you check to see if they had stock?"

"They do," Del said. "I took a look inside."

"How many men?"

"Only one," Del said. "There's about a half a dozen horses in a corral out back."

"Trail-worthy stock?" Dutch asked. Del was a good boy, but he wasn't the best judge of horseflesh.

"They looked okay to me."

Dutch didn't really care how good the horses were. They only needed them to get on the trail. Once they left the city lim-its, he figured they'd be able to find a small ranch they could raid for better stock.

"Saddles?"

"They got some tack inside," Del said, "but I couldn't tell how much."

"Pa," Coy said, "you know we can ride bareback."

"You might have to, for a while," Dutch said, "but only un-til we get on the move."

"So," Luke asked, "are we gonna do this?"

"We're gonna do it," Dutch said, "but Sam is gonna go and get us some supplies."

"Steal 'em?" Sam asked, hopefully.

"Buy 'em," Dutch said. "Just enough to get us started. Put it all in a sack and then get back here. By then we'll have the horses ready to go."

"Aw, Pa," Sam said, "why can't I—"

"Keep your gun in your holster, boy," Dutch said. He took some money from his pocket—what he had left from St. Louis—and handed it to Sam. "Don't mess up."

"I won't, Pa."

"Then go."

As Sam walked, Dutch turned to the others and said, "Let's do this."

It was the next morning when Sheriff Brody was called to that livery stable.

"See, Carl?" Ben Collins told him. "I told you."

Brody walked in and looked down at the body of the owner, Ray Toller. He'd been shot in the chest.

"One shot," Brody said. "Around here that'd go unnoticed." This area was dying off, and Toller was one of the last merchants hanging on, probably because he couldn't afford to move.

"I came in to open up, and there he was," Ben complained. "Scared me to death."

"Go look out back, Ben," Brody said. "Tell me what you see."

Collins walked out behind the stable, then came back. Brody was crouched over Toller's body.

"So?"

"There's one horse in the corral, Carl."

"And how many were there yesterday?"

"Six."

"Can you tell if he rented any out?"

"We usually makes a note in a book in the back." Collins went to take a look. "He didn't make no note, Ben."

"Okay," Brody said, "he was shot, and the horses were stolen. Anything else missing?"

Collins looked around.

"Two saddles and some bridles and blankets, looks like."

"Somebody outfitted themselves for free," Brody said. "You better call the city police. They'll have somebody come and pick up the body."

"What about you?"

"I'm gonna get a head start on findin' out who did this."

"How you gonna do that?"

"By checking the train station and seeing if five men got off together."

"Why five?"

Brody stared at Collins.

"Because, Ben," he said, slowly, "that's how many horses were stolen."

FORTY-TWO

By the middle of the next day Dutch and his boys found what they were looking for, an isolated little spread outside of Ardmore with horses in a corral.

"Those horses are better than these nags," Dutch said. "I can see that from here."

"Good," Coy said, "then I can have my own horse again."

The sticks they'd stolen in Oklahoma City had been so bad that Coy's had died right under him, and he was now riding double with Sam.

Dutch and Luke were the two using saddles, while the others rode bareback.

"We'd better check the area, see if there are any hands around," Dutch said. "If not, then we'll go in. We'll want whatever we can find—horses, saddles, supplies from the house. Maybe even some money."

They had gotten a few dollars from the livery where they'd stolen the horses, but not much. It had been in a perfect location for them to rob, but had not yielded anything really worth stealing.

"Okay, boys," Dutch said. "Scout around and meet back here in fifteen minutes. Then we'll go in."

By the start of the third day they had decent horses beneath them, enough supplies to hold them for a while, and—

169

counting Ray Toller—they'd only had to kill three people to
get it all.

By the end of the third day—the same night Clint and
Rachel made their five-thousand-dollar bargain—Dave
Cole came riding into the camp made by the Tanner and his
men.

"It's about time," Tanner said. "I thought you got lost."

"I didn't get lost," Cole said, "but I found—"

"Wait," Tanner said. He called one of the other men over
and had him take Cole's horse. "Come over here." He pulled
Cole away from the others.

"I found where they camped last night," Cole said. "Definitely two people, two horses and a buckboard."

Tanner couldn't have been happier, because he'd managed
to lose the trail halfway through the day.

"How far off course are we?" he asked.

"About a day."

"Can you get us back on the right trail," he asked, "without
them finding out?"

"We could just tell 'em—"

"I think it's better if they think we know what we're doing,
Dave," Tanner said, "don't you?"

"Yes, sir."

"Okay," Tanner said. "In the morning you'll take the lead
and steer us over into the right direction."

"Yes, sir."

"Go get yourself something to eat. You did a good job."

He watched Cole go over to the fire where the other men
were gathered. They slapped him on the back, laughing, and
handed him a plate of food and some coffee. Tanner hoped
they weren't so friendly that Cole would tell them what was
going on. He needed the respect of these men, and he would
have hated to find out they were laughing behind his back.

He would have hated it with a passion.

As they headed out the fourth day, Clint and Rachel had no
idea of the blood that had been shed since they left Oklahoma
City, and they had no idea that there was not only one group,

but two on their trail, with generally the same thought in mind: catch up to them.

And kill them.

But for five thousand dollars, Clint Adams was prepared to handle whatever came along.

FORTY-THREE

Sheriff Brody sat in a chair in the captain's office, staring across the desk at Dale Jennings. He'd had many run-ins with the captain and considered the man to be a politician, not a peace officer.

"So what do you want to do, Sheriff?"

"It's not what I want to do, Captain," Brody said, "it's what I'm going to do."

"And what's that?"

"Put a posse together and go after these five men," the sheriff said.

"And do you know who the five men are?"

"I have a description," Brody said. "I also have information that they were looking for Roy Frump."

"Frump?"

"He and the two brothers, Keenan and Bobo Miller, were killed at the station by Clint Adams and Rachel Chandler."

"Ah," Jennings said, "the infamous Gunsmith."

"I think they're on his trail."

"Looking for revenge, are they?"

"Possibly."

"Well then," the captain said, "that's business between them, isn't it?"

"They killed Ray Toller, and stole five horses," Brody said. "I think that makes it our business."

"Very well, Sheriff," Jennings said. "What do you want me to do?"

"Send some men with me," Brody said. "We'll have a joint posse. My deputies and your men. You can even send that . . . Sergeant Tanner you like so much."

"Tanner is on another assignment," Jennings said, "and, in fact, he has with him the only men I could spare."

"So you won't send anyone?"

"I think you're perfectly capable of handling this, Sheriff," Jennings said. "After all, this is the city police. I can't imagine my men out there on horseback as part of a posse, can you?"

"Actually," Brody said, standing up, "no, I can't. This was just a courtesy call."

"Well then," Jennings said, "I appreciate the courtesy."

He looked down at his desk, the gesture a clear one of dismissal. Brody actually didn't mind it. He truly did not want any of Jennings's men with him, especially that idiot of the East, Tanner.

Still, as he left the police station, he couldn't help but wonder what special assignment Tanner would be on that required him to take so many men.

FORTY-FOUR

Toward the end of day four, Clint was able to keep his promise to Rachel about her bath. They came across a water hole that was deep enough for her to swim in.

"Can we stop?" she asked, her eyes lighting up. "Can we afford to stop?"

"I don't see why not," he said. "I'll keep watch while you swim and clean your clothes."

"Oh no," she said. "If I'm taking a bath, so are you. What good is it going to do for me not to stink if I can still smell you?"

Clint lifted his sleeve to his nose and sniffed.

"Maybe you don't smell you," she told him, "but I do."

"Well, all right," he said, "but you first, because someone has to stand watch."

"Okay."

He watched as she unabashedly stripped down to her underthings, but when he saw that she was obviously going to remove those, as well, he averted his eyes until he head a splash, telling him she was in the water. When he looked, he could only see her from the shoulders up.

"Such a gentleman," she said, "although I don't know why, after the other night."

"Old habits die hard."

"This feels so wonderful," she said. "It's warm, but it still feels good. You should come in with me."

"Rachel—"

She swam toward the shore so she could stand up. Her black hair was plastered to her head. The water ran off her body as she stood, and her skin gleamed. Her heavy breasts looked even larger when they were wet, and he felt his body responding to her. She came a little closer to shore, and he could see her deep belly button, and then the wet patch of hair between her legs.

"Come on, Clint," she said, cupping the undersides of her breasts with her hands, "it's only a bath. It won't take long."

"You're going to get us killed," he muttered, but started to undress.

Naked, he got in the water with her. She'd moved back out to where it was deep, so he swam out to join her and took her in his arms. He kissed her, crushing her to him, running his hands over her. Sliding one hand between them he touched her, moving one finger over her, and then in and out of her while she made little noises of pleasure. She put her hands on his shoulders as if trying to climb him, trying to ride his finger as if it were his cock. Finally he took hold of her by her buttocks and drew her back closer to shore with him so he could stand. Once his feet were firmly planted beneath him, he lifted her onto his penis. She gasped as he entered her, and then she began to bob up and down on him, her head thrown back. He bit her breasts hard, causing her to gasp again, from pain or pleasure or a combination of the two. At that point it really didn't matter. She was right about the water, it was lukewarm, but her insides were steaming hot. She pulled herself to him so she could kiss him while they continued to fuck. She was a big woman, and he felt the pressure in his legs and thighs, but it felt good. They continued that way, splashing about, both gasping and grunting, until she suddenly shuddered and clasped herself to him tightly, as she rode the waves of pleasure washing over her, and then he could hold back no longer. He bellowed out his own pleasure as he emptied himself into her; then he slid from her so they could drift away from each other, catching their breath . . .

• • •

"See?" she said, minutes later. "We're not dead."

They were out of the water and dressing and Clint was looking around them anxiously.

"Just because we're lucky," he said.

He looked at the sky and said, "We might as well camp here. By the time we get ready to leave, it will almost be dusk."

"Suits me," she said. "You can build a fire while I wash some clothes, and then I'll make something to eat. Don't button that shirt."

He turned and found her looking at him.

"I'll wash it with the others."

"Okay," he said. "I'll get a clean one."

He walked to his horse, pulled a clean shirt out and exchanged it for the dirty one.

"Give it to me," she said, coming up behind him. "I'll start washing right away. By the time I'm done, you should have a fire going."

"All right," Clint said, "but before you start washing the clothes, fill the canteens."

"Right."

As Rachel went back to the water hole with an armful of clothes—mostly hers—Clint collected wood and got the fire going. By the time Rachel returned from the fire, the sun had dried her hair, and was going down.

"I hope we have enough sun left to dry the clothes tonight," she said.

"Won't matter," he said. "They'll probably dry overnight."

"Bacon and beans?" she asked.

"Sounds fine," he said, "as long as it's accompanied by a lot of strong coffee."

"First thing."

"Let me have your gun," he said. "I'll clean it and your rifle."

"Thank you."

"Just returning the favor."

While she cooked, Clint sat nearby and cleaned the weapons, all the while keeping an eye out.

"It's been four days," she said. "You still think somebody is coming after us?"

"We're safer if we keep thinking that way."

She thought a moment, then said, "I guess I can't argue with that kind of logic."

She picked up the coffeepot, filled a cup and carried it to him.

"I noticed something about you."

"You did?" he asked. "What? When?"

"Today," she said. "The entire day, you never looked at the coffin. Not once."

"So?"

"Why is that? Not curious anymore?"

"No, I'm not."

"And what are your reasons for that?"

"I have five thousand reasons for that."

"So this is just a job now?"

"Yes."

"So if I offered you a look in the coffin now, and I'd still paid you five thousand dollars, what would you say?"

"I'd say no."

"Well then . . ."

She turned and walked back to the fire. He knew what she was doing with her "Well, then . . ." She was trying to see if all of his curiosity was gone. She wanted him to say, "Well then . . . what?"

He wasn't about to play her games, though.

"I'm going to take a walk around," he said, "before dark. I might spot something."

"The food'll be ready in five minutes."

"There's a small hill a few hundred yards back," he said. "I'll just walk there and back."

"Suit yourself."

By the time he topped the hill, half his coffee was gone, and most of the sun. He could still see a long way off, and there was no sign of a horse and rider, no sign of a dust cloud that would indicate motion. Four days. If someone was coming, wouldn't they have caught up by now? Especially since he and Rachel were hauling a coffin in the bed of the buckboard.

Up to now, both times they'd been attacked had been at a train station. Since Roy Frump had claimed this was a family matter, he must have been related to . . . somebody. Maybe there were more family members involved, waiting at train stations down the line, between Oklahoma City and Austin. Maybe he and Rachel were in the clear as long as they stayed away from railway stations.

He started walking back to the campfire.

FORTY-FIVE

Fully outfitted, the Crater men and Del Crockett were camped several days behind Clint and Rachel that same night. Dutch felt all they had to do now was head due south toward Austin, and they'd eventually catch up to Rachel and her protector.

"What about cousin Floyd?" Luke asked.

"What about him?"

"Ain't he gonna be waitin' at the train station in Austin?"

"Sure he is." Dutch said. "Waitin' and waitin'. He'll wait there until either we get there, or until Rachel gets off a train."

"You think she's still gonna take a train?" Del asked.

"They might stop someplace like Dallas, or Fort Worth, and catch another train. Either way, we'll catch up to them."

Del handed Dutch a tin plate of food. Both the plate and the food had been stolen from the ranch, where they'd left two people dead.

"Won't be for a couple of days," Dutch added, "but we'll catch up to her, and her hired gun."

Coy looked around the fire at his brothers, his father and Del, and said, "I don't know about you fellas, but I ain't lookin' forward to facin' this fella she's got with her."

The others remained silent, and Luke actually leaned away from his brother.

"What?" Dutch asked.

"Well, I mean, ain't he supposed to be a fast gun?" Coy

asked. "Ain't none of us fast guns. Look what he did to Magellan—and to Uncle Roy and those other two? No, sir, I sure don't wanna face him—"

He was cut off by a vicious backhand from his father which sent him ass over teakettle, his plate of food flying in the other direction.

"What the hell—" he said, righting himself and holding his jaw.

"Your brother Billy is dead," Dutch said, standing up, "and we're gonna do whatever it takes to see that his killer pays."

"What the hell," Coy said, again. "This fella didn't kill him!"

"But if he gets in our way," Dutch said, "he's gonna pay for it. I don't care how fast he is or how big his reputation is. You got that?"

"Well, yeah, Pa, but—"

"No buts, Coy," Dutch said. "Me and your brothers are gonna be countin' on you to do your part. If you ain't gonna do it, tell me right now. Look at them and tell them!"

Coy dropped his hand from his jaw and looked around at his brothers, and at Del Crockett.

"Okay, okay," he said, "I'm gonna do my part. I never said I wasn't. I just said I wasn't lookin' forward to it. Jeez, ya didn't have ta hit me!"

"Shut up," Dutch said. "Sit down and finish eatin'."

Dutch sat himself back down, and waited for Coy to do the same.

"Del, give Coy another plate."

Camped between Clint and Rachel, and the Crater bunch, was Sergeant Dan Tanner and his men. Tanner was feeling better about things. Cole had been able to subtly get them back on the trail, and now he sure they were heading in the right direction.

Tanner chose to eat apart from the "enlisted men." He'd decided to run this "posse" like a military unit. He was in command, and Cole would be his second. To that end, Cole was allowed to come over and have a cup of coffee with him.

"Do you think they know?" Cole asked.

"Know what?"

"What I was doing all day."

"No," Tanner said, "they don't know. You did a good job. They never suspected a thing."

"I hope not," Cole said.

"Cole," Tanner said, "I want to talk to you about the chain of command . . ."

Cal Barnes, Howard Teal and Steve McNally sat around the fire, watching Tanner and Cole converse just on the edge of the light.

"Whataya think they're talkin' about?" Barnes asked

"Probably tryin' to figure out where we are," Teal said. "Them two is hopelessly lost."

"If that's true," McNally said, "then we're lost, too."

"Who cares?" Teal asked. "At least we ain't back in Oklahoma City, workin'."

"Yeah," Barnes said, "but what do we do if we do catch up to Clint Adams?"

"Clint Adams," McNally said. "There's a real name from the Old West."

"He ain't so old," Barnes said. "Not from what I hear."

"If we do catch up," Teal said, "do you think Tanner was serious about what we're supposed to do?"

"What's that?"

"Weren't you listenin'?" McNally asked. "We're supposed to bring him back dead."

Teal stared at McNally. "No, we ain't."

"Yeah," Barnes said, "we are."

Teal stared at Barnes.

"No, we ain't."

"We are," McNally said.

"He didn't say that."

"You gotta read between the lines, Howie," Barnes said. "The boss wants him dead."

"Jesus," Teal said. "I didn't know that."

"You agreed to come along," McNally reminded him.

"Yeah, but . . . I didn't know we was supposed to . . . murder the Gunsmith."

"We ain't supposed to murder nobody," Barnes said. "We just gotta bring him to justice, ya know? He killed some people."

"He's the Gunsmith," Teal said. "He's supposed to kill people. That's his job."

"Well, it's our job to stop him, then," McNally said.

"Before we stop him," Barnes said, "we're gonna have to find him."

Teal looked over to where Tanner and Cole were still talking.

"Those two is hopelessly lost."

This time, he hoped he was right.

Camped alone, behind the Crater bunch, was Sheriff Carl Brody. The lawman had given himself two choices—he could take the time to put together a posse, or he could head out alone and try to catch up to the killers of Ray Toller.

Brody had studied the ground in the corral and had found something interesting. One of the horses had a distinctive hoofprint, and as long as the killers had that horse, the trail would lead him right to them.

When he did catch up to them, that's when he'd worry about not having a posse with him.

FORTY-SIX

Rachel woke the next morning reborn.

"Having clean clothes does that for a woman," she explained to Clint over breakfast.

"Just clean clothes?" he asked.

She smiled at him. They had each taken a watch again during the night, so they had also each slept alone. And while Clint had thoroughly enjoyed his "bath" with Rachel, he was determined that there would be no further "bathing" until they reached Austin.

As far as clothes went, there was no way Clint would ever try to understand women. Sometimes clean—and new—clothes were annoying to a man, especially a man who spent time on a horse. They chafed, or itched, and they did not move with a man until he had worn them for some time and broken them in.

But he decided not to try to explain this to her.

"Here," she said, handing him the shirt she had washed for him the day before.

"Thank you."

He walked to his saddlebags, balled the shirt up and stuffed it into one of them. When he turned, she was staring at him.

"What?"

"I washed that for you," she said. "You're not going to put it on?"

"Not right now," he said. "This shirt is fine."

"But . . . you rolled it up into a ball."

"The shirt will be fine, Rachel," he said. "When I need a clean one, I'll take it out and put it on."

"And when do you think that would be?" she asked. "I mean, you got washed yesterday, you really should put a clean shirt on—"

He held up his hand and said, "Remember what I said about us getting along? Besides, this is a clean shirt."

Clint went to work saddling one horse and hitching the other to the buckboard. By the time he was done, Rachel had broken camp, doused the fire and was ready to go.

"Can I ride today?" she asked.

"Sure," Clint said. "Why not?"

He watched as with no help from him she mounted the horse and gathered up the reins. She sat the horse competently and confidently.

"Nice animal," she said. "It's been a while since I've been on a horse."

"You look like a natural."

"Thank you."

Clint climbed aboard the buckboard and gathered up the reins.

"Shall we go?" he asked. "Don't ride too far ahead of me," he instructed her.

"Are you afraid I'll fall off?"

"I'm being paid to protect you," he said. "I won't be able to do that if you get too far ahead."

"Of course. I'll just ride alongside."

As they started out, she asked, "How much longer do you think it will be before we get to Austin?"

"It's going to take at least five more days, maybe six," he replied. "There should be more opportunities between here and there for you to swim, though."

"I never expected this when I agreed—" she started, but she stopped short.

"Agreed to . . . what?"

"It doesn't matter," she said. "Are you sure we can't stop somewhere along the way and catch a train for the rest of the trip? I mean, there can't be someone waiting for us at every train station."

"Maybe not," Clint said, "but from the way things have gone so far, I'm sure there will be someone waiting for us at the station in Austin . . . don't you think?"

"I suppose," she said, grudgingly.

"You're paying me to see that you and your . . . husband's coffin . . . get to Austin safely, and that's what I'm going to do, Rachel. This is the best way I can see to do it."

"You're right," she said. "I'm just being . . . petty."

They rode along in silence for a while before Rachel broke the quiet. She turned her head and looked at him from beneath the brim of her Stetson, which was shielding her eyes from the sun.

"I find you a very strange man."

"Stranger than most?"

"Wonderful . . . but stranger than any," she said. "I can't figure out why you approached me in St. Louis in the first place."

He hesitated just for a moment, then said, "You know what? Neither can I."

FORTY-SEVEN

Sheriff Carl Brody knew who had lived in the small spread just outside of Ardmore in Oklahoma Territory. He thought about them as he rode south through Texas.

The man's name had been Gary Truscott, and he'd had a wife and a son. The boy had been six when the man died after being kicked in the head by a horse. The woman, Gayle, decided to stay there and live, trying to make the spread work, rather than taking the boy, Mark, and moving into a town or a city. For six years she worked, and when the boy got old enough he had become a great help. The two of them were very close to making the spread a going concern, but three or four men—maybe more—had ridden up on them, killed them both and looted the place. Behind they left an empty corral and a burned-out shell of a house, and that was what Sheriff Brody had found when he rode up on the place.

Brody had met the family for the first time while riding with a posse almost ten years before, and from time to time he had found himself near the place and would stop in for a drink, or a meal, or to water his horse. After Gary's death, he'd stop in from time to time to see how Gayle and Mark were doing.

This time he found the charred corpses of Gayle and Mark in the fire. He only hoped the men had shot them before torching the house, rather than burning them alive.

189

There was nothing he could have done for them, and pausing to bury the remains, or going into Ardmore to report what had happened to the law there, would have put him farther behind these men. He hated to do it, but he had to leave them where they lay and continue on. He took a moment to say a prayer, and then left.

The problem he faced now was that the killers had switched horses at the Truscott place and had run off the horses they'd stolen from Ray Toller, including the one with the distinctive hoofprint. They were now riding horses that bore the three T's of the Truscott brand. Their trail leaving the ranch was clear, but Brody didn't know how long it would stay that way.

He had a theory, though. He thought that these killers, since they had asked after Roy Frump at the train station, were actually after Clint Adams and the woman, Rachel Chandler. He recalled Clint telling him that he and Mrs. Chandler were heading for Austin. In the event Brody lost the trail left by these bastards, he intended to simply continue south, even if he had to ride clear to Austin before he finally caught up to the men. Whether there were four or five—and he would have known for sure had he been a better reader of signs—he was going to bring them to justice for what they had done to Ray Toller, and to Gayle Truscott and her twelve-year-old son— and he was talking about old-fashioned justice, the kind that came from the barrel of a gun.

FORTY-EIGHT

There were four campfires strung out in a straight line each night for the next couple of days, and each night they were a little closer together.

The slowest travelers were Clint and Rachel, followed by Sergeant Tanner and his men.

The riders who were moving the quickest were the Crater bunch and Sheriff Carl Brody.

Because Brody was traveling alone, he was able to move the quickest of all. He broke camp faster, and got an earlier start each day than all the others. He noticed that the trail he was following, rather than growing fainter as he'd feared, was getting clearer and clearer. In fact, coming across one of the men's campfires, he was finally able to determine for sure that there were five of them. That didn't deter him, though. Seeing that he was getting closer only caused him to become more excited. It had been a while since he'd tracked a gang he wanted so badly he could taste it.

Tanner, who had been frustrated for the past few days, was now growing excited. According to Cole they were actually getting closer and closer. Last night's campfire, Cole said, actually still had some heat in the ashes.

"We're not that far behind," he told Tanner.

"Tell the men to be ready," Tanner instructed him. "As soon as we come up on them, I'm going to want to move."

"Yes, sir."

Cole went back to relay the message to the other men.

"Hey, Cole," Barnes called.

"Yeah?"

"Do you really know what you're doin'?"

Cole, who hadn't been so sure himself until he found this recent campfire, said, "Yeah, Barnes, I do."

"Does he?" McNally asked.

Cole turned to see where Tanner was before he answered. He didn't want the sergeant to hear him.

"I don't know about that, McNally," he said, lowering his voice. "I only know he's in charge."

"Hey, Cole, are we really supposed to . . . ya know, kill this fella Clint?" Teal asked.

"That's what the sergeant said, Teal."

Teal sat back in his saddle and said, "Damn."

"This campfire is different," Del Crockett told Dutch.

"Whataya mean, different?"

"You can tell," Del said, pointing. "More people sittin' around this one."

"So what's that mean?"

"One of two things," Del said. "We're crossing paths with some other group that ain't involved, or . . ."

"Or somebody else is followin' Clint Adams and Rachel," Luke finished.

"Right," Del said.

Dutch looked around at the other faces.

"Who else would be trackin' them?"

"Well . . . ," Del said.

"Well what, Del?" Dutch asked. "Spit it out."

"It's just that they killed three men in Oklahoma City," Del reminded them.

"You think there's a posse on their trail?"

"Could be," Del said, with a shrug.

"He might be right, Pa," Luke said.

"What if he is?" Sam asked. "What if we run into a posse, Pa?"

"We'll handle 'em, that's what," Dutch said. "This is about family. I ain't lettin' no posse stop us." He looked down at Del, the only one of them who had dismounted. "Get back on your horse, boy. We're movin' out."

Carl Brody also found the different campfires and realized what was going on. It was the only answer. Jennings— ambitious, amoral Captain Jennings—must have sent Sergeant Dan Tanner after Clint Adams and the woman. Meanwhile, the killers were also following the trail. All of this made sense to Brody because, without it, these campfires set in a line that pointed south would be a coincidence.

Brody started to wonder what he should do: increase his pace to try to catch up with the killers, or simply follow along and wait for all their trails to intersect? He could certainly use the help of Tanner and his men with the killers. The only problem was that he had no confidence in anyone who was connected to a police department who would put a man like Jennings in a position of authority.

Maybe the best thing for him to do was catch the killers around their campfire, get the drop on them when they were eating. If he could disarm them, he could get them to tie each other up. Then all he'd have to do was get them mounted and ride them back to Oklahoma City.

But what about Clint Adams? After all, his killing of those three men was justified. Could he just allow Tanner and his men to track him, arrest him and bring him back to stand trial on a trumped-up charge? Then again, he had a witness, the woman who was with him. And still again, she had pulled the trigger on one of the men. Jennings probably intended to put her on trial, too. Pinning a murder charge on a legend of the Old West like the Gunsmith would be a feather in his political cap. Of course, that meant that Clint Adams would have to be convicted.

On the other hand, why would Jennings take a chance like that? What if Clint Adams were apprehended on the trail and . . . killed before he could be brought back?

Could Brody afford to just let that happen? After all, his responsibility was the killers, not Clint, and not Dan Tanner.

But he had a greater responsibility than even that—a responsibility to his own conscience.

FORTY-NINE

They were between Waco and Austin—maybe a day and a half out of Austin—when Clint spotted them.

They had just negotiated a steep hill, the horse struggling to get the buckboard to the top, so they stopped there to give the animal a rest. Clint turned in his seat and looked behind them and didn't like what he saw.

"We've got to move," he told Rachel.

She looked over at him from astride the saddle horse and said, "I thought we needed to rest the hor—"

"We can rest at the bottom of the hill," Clint said, cutting her off. "Come on."

He started off down the other side of the hill, and had to use the brake judiciously to keep the buckboard from actually shoving the horse along. At the bottom Rachel rode over to him.

"What's going on?"

"Switch with me," he said. "Come on!"

She moved the horse over next to him so they could switch places without either of them touching the ground.

"Clint—"

"I saw some riders," he said, "and if I saw them, they might have seen us. I want you to keep going and I'll catch up."

"What if you don't?"

195

"Then keep going until you hit Austin," he said, "and keep both of your guns handy."

"Clint—"

"Don't worry," he said. "I'm just going to ride back and get a look at them, see if I recognize anybody."

"Be careful,"

He nodded, and then headed around the hill rather than going back up . . .

"What was that?" Cole asked.

Tanner, who'd been looking down at the ground, lifted his head and asked, "What?"

"I thought I saw something up ahead," Cole said.

"Where?"

"Straight ahead."

Tanner looked and saw nothing.

"It's gone," Cole said.

"Or maybe there was never anything there," Tanner said, dejectedly. "Cole, I think you've got us totally lost."

"We're not lost, Sergeant," Cole said. "Austin is dead ahead, two days, maybe less."

"Well, maybe that's not where they're going."

Tanner was feeling more frustration than ever. Trailing Clint Adams and the woman for eight days was much more than he'd bargained for. They should have caught up to them by now. If they had to engage Adams in Austin, they'd have to deal with the local law. They'd have to take him and head back with him before he could carry out his orders to the letter. Catching up to him and the woman on the trail would have made everything so much simpler. No other law to worry about, and no witnesses.

"All right," he said, "let's just keep going . . ."

As Dutch spotted Del Crockett riding back to them, he reined his horse in and called their progress to a halt. His sons stopped behind him, but Coy's horse ran into the back of Sam's because Coy had been asleep in his addle.

"They're up ahead," Del said.

"Rachel?"

"No," Del said, "looks like a posse."

"How many?"

"Five."

"Odds are even," Dutch said, "but we have surprise on our side." He turned in his saddle. "Boys. Check your guns!"

Carl Brody reined his horse in and stared. Ahead of him he could see five riders clumped together. They were close enough to see, but out of rifle range. If he rode hard, he could reach them fairly quickly, but he could not reach them without them hearing him coming. He was going to have to close on them without them noticing, and then follow them until nightfall, when they camped. That was when he would be able to surprise them.

What he didn't realize was that there were a lot of surprises to come before that.

Rachel drove on while Clint turned his horse and went back. Was she close enough to make Austin alone, if Clint didn't return? She certainly would prefer not to have to try.

She grabbed her rifle and put it on the seat next to her. Her stomach was in knots now. Something she hadn't told Clint was that when she put her derringer to the side of Roy Frump's head and pulled the trigger, that was the first time she had ever killed anyone. She'd done it because she felt she didn't have a choice, but she didn't like it, and she was hoping not to have to do it again.

She'd hoped to have Clint Adams do all the killing from that point on—and she still did.

FIFTY

Clint, riding back toward the Oklahoma City posse, was about the same distance from them as Brody—riding forward—was from the Crater bunch. So when the first shots were fired, they were equally as loud to both of them, and spurred them each on. However, when they came within sight of the action, they were so intent on what was happening that they did not see each other.

The first move was made by Dutch Crater and his boys.

They were able to close the ground between them and the posse by splitting up and coming at them from opposite directions. Dutch formulated the plan, took Sam with him and sent Coy with Luke and Del Crockett.

"We get 'em between us and catch 'em in a cross fire," he explained to them.

"What do we do if they hear us comin'?" Coy asked.

"I don't care if they hear us," Dutch said. "We just keep comin' at 'em, understand? And come shootin'!"

Cole heard them first, looked to his left and saw two riders coming at them.

"Sergeant."

"What?" Tanner asked, still annoyed with the whole situation.

"Riders comin' at us fast from the east."

"What?" Tanner said, again. He turned his head and saw the two men coming toward them. "What do they want?"

"Maybe they need help," Cole said. "It's two men, not a man and a woman, so . . ."

"And no buckboard," Tanner said.

"Riders, Sergeant!" Barnes suddenly shouted.

"We see them, Barnes—"

"No," Barnes shouted, "from the west."

"Wha—" Tanner turned his head and saw three more riders coming from the opposite directions.

"What do we do, Sergeant?" McNally called out.

If they had been a real military unit, they would have been on the defensive immediately, anticipating trouble. Instead, Tanner froze, unsure of what to do next. Were these men a threat?

His question was answered with a bullet.

Dutch's instructions had been for no one to fire until he did. He waited until the men saw them coming, then lifted his rifle, picked one out and fired. His bullet struck home and plucked the man from his saddle. With that, the others began firing as well. It occurred to Dutch that this could not have been a very experienced posse—not judging from the way they reacted— and now they'd never have the chance to learn.

The first bullet took Barnes in the neck, knocking him off his horse. He was still alive when he hit the ground, but found that he couldn't move, not even a finger. In the next moment his spooked horse stamped down on his head, killing him instantly.

A barrage of shots followed. The horses began dancing about, some of them spooked, some of them hit by hot lead. Tanner's horse went down, crushing his leg beneath its weight. A bullet hit McNally in the side, then hit his horse in the neck. They both went down, but he was able to roll free before the animal's weight could crush him.

Teal and Cole had time to draw their guns, but before they could find targets they were hit by two bullets each. Cole felt one poke through his side, and another hit him in the knee.

Teal was struck in the arm first, and as a quick thought went to his brain to switch his gun to his other hand, a bullet took its place a split second later. It came out the other side of his head, taking most of his brain with it.

In moments all the men were down, as were some of the horses, the others running off.

And it was over.

Clint felt helpless as he looked down at the scene of the slaughter. He could have fired down from his vantage point on a hill. He was lying on his belly, and he could probably pick two of the assailants off before they located him. But his job was to get Rachel Chandler to Austin, and he could do no good for the five dead men, whoever they were.

Then he noticed that one man was still alive, struggling as he was pinned beneath the weight of his horse.

Brody was in a similar position as Clint Adams, lying on his belly with his rifle ready, staring down at the scene. Like Clint, he knew he could probably take a couple of the men out quick, but that would give away his position. He chose to watch, and wait. He also saw the man struggling beneath his horse, but unlike Clint he recognized him as Sergeant Dan Tanner.

If Clint and Brody had known about each other, and had fired at the same time, they probably could have cut down the entire Crater bunch, but they didn't. Clint chose to back away and ride back to Rachel to tell her what had happened.

Brody chose to just lie there, watch and wait.

Dan Tanner stared up at the men pointing guns at him, his body wracked with pain. His leg had been crushed by the weight of the horse. Had he been in the city, a doctor probably could have saved the leg. Out here, if he had been dragged from beneath the horse, the leg would have had to be amputated.

Neither of those things was going to happen, though . . .

"Should we ask him who he is, Pa?" Luke asked.

"No," Dutch said. "We can find that out by going through his saddlebags."

"Then what do we do with him?" Coy asked.

"Kill him," Dutch said, "Now."

Dutch turned and walked away.

"Which one of u—" Coy began to ask, but he was too late. Both Luke and Del fired at the same time . . .

Tanner was scared, but he was in so much pain that when the two men fired at him and he felt the bullets hit him, he figured it was for the best.

At least nothing hurt anymore . . .

FIFTY-ONE

When Rachel heard the horse coming behind her, she hunched her shoulders. She considered whipping her own horse into a run, but she'd never be able to outrun anyone. Not with the coffin in the back. She reined the horse in, grabbed her rifle and turned, and relief flooded her when she saw that it was Clint.

"What happened?" she asked, when he reached her. "I thought I heard shots."

"You did." He rode his horse right up alongside of her, so she was able to lower her rifle and sit back down.

"What was it?"

"A slaughter," he said, and explained what he saw.

"Did you try to help them?"

"There was nothing I could have done," he said. "By the time I got there, they were all down." Not all dead, but he wasn't going to tell her that. He knew that the survivor trapped beneath his horse was not going to last very long.

"My God," she asked. "Who were they?"

"Which group?" he asked. "One of the groups was probably after us. Which one, I don't know, but I'm going to guess the second group."

"Why?"

"The second group slaughtered the first mercilessly," he said. "They were killers, and that's who's after us, right?"

She didn't answer.

"Right, Rachel?" He reached out and grabbed her arm. "It's time for you to tell me who these people are." He pointed with the other arm. "They're not that far behind us. The longer we sit here, the closer they get."

He doubted that was the case. He was sure the men would first loot what they could from the dead bodies. Money, weapons, supplies. That would give them a little time to work with.

Time for her to finally tell him what was going on.

Brody felt sick to his stomach, but at least he knew that these were the same men who had killed Gayle Truscott and her son. They had to be. He hated to think that there were two bands of men this ruthless riding around out here.

He watched as the killers systematically searched the dead bodies and the horses, and took what they wanted. Abruptly, he heard a horse to his right, and he turned that way, rifle ready. It was a riderless horse, belonging to one on the posse, no doubt. He got up and approached the animal, which stood fast. He grabbed the reins, swung the horse around and saw the Truscott brand. That sealed it. These were, indeed, the same men who had burned the Truscott place to the ground, and now they had killed five Oklahoma City policemen.

There wasn't much Brody could do at the moment, except continue to watch, and follow, and wait. He released the horse, which trotted away a few yards and then stopped. It would probably make its way back to the burned-out Truscott place, if someone didn't find it and claim it first. He'd given brief thought to taking what he might need from it, but was afraid that would make him as bad as the killers, so he took nothing.

He watched as the men finished with the dead lawmen and mounted up. One of them gave a brief look back his way, but he had removed his hat and could not be seen from down where they were.

He waited.

"Got everything?" Dutch asked.

"They had a little bit of money each, Pa," Luke said, "and a rifle and handgun each."

"That's an extra rifle and handgun for each of us."

"No, we only got three rifles," Del said. "Two of the horses ran off."

"Want us to run the horses down, Pa?" Coy asked.

"No," Dutch said. "We don't need 'em. What else did they have on 'em, Luke?"

"Some beef jerky; one of them was carrying some coffee. They was traveling light like we was."

"And they had these," Del said. He opened his hand and showed Dutch five Oklahoma City Police badges.

Dutch started laughing.

"Well," he said, through the laughter, "these might come in handy if we do end up in Austin. Everybody take one and put it in your pocket. Don't put it on unless I say."

"Here," Del said, handing one to Dutch. "It's a sergeant's badge. He was in command, I guess."

"Thanks," Dutch said, accepting it. He put it in his shirt pocket. "Everybody get mounted."

Dutch climbed astride his horse and waited for the others to do the same. He looked off into the distance, wondering if Rachel and Clint were close enough to have heard the shots. He hoped they were. It would start them thinking, worrying.

Luke rode up alongside him and said, "We're ready, Pa."

Coy let out a whoop that got all of their attention and announced, "That was fun!"

Dutch looked at Luke, who shrugged.

"That boy's an idiot," Dutch said.

FIFTY-TWO

"Come on, Rachel." Clint looked back. "I could be wrong; they could be right behind us."

"Well then, let's move!"

"Not until you tell me something."

She glared at him.

"Your curiosity is up again, now?" she asked. "Do you want to look inside the coffin?"

"I don't care what's in the coffin," he said. "I doubt it's a body, because embalmed or not it would be stinking to high heaven by now."

"Then what do you want?"

"I want to know who's chasing us, Rachel," he said. "Who wants you dead so bad they'd follow us halfway across the country—or, at least, Texas?"

"Clint," she said, "really, I—"

"They could be coming over that rise any minute."

"All right!" she said. "Fine. You want to know who's chasing us? I'll tell you."

Instead, she started biting her lip.

"I'm waiting."

She mumbled something.

"What?"

"I said it's my father," she shouted. "Okay? My father and my brothers."

207

She explained that a man named Dutch Crater was her father, and that she had four brothers.

"Living with them was hell," she said, "especially after my mother died. I had to become a mother to all of them—even to Luke, the oldest. And I had to become a wife to my pa."

"A wife?" Clint asked. "Did he—"

"No!" she said. "But that's about the only thing he didn't do to me—and he kept my brothers from doing it to me, too. But he wanted me to marry my brother Luke's best friend, Del Crockett, and he's just as bad as my brothers."

"So?"

"So I married the first man who asked me," she said, "and that was Ethan Chandler. He was my father's age, but I didn't care about that. I thought it would get me away from him, and from my brothers, and . . ."

"And what?"

"And he had money," she said. "But you know what? He turned out to be a lot like my father."

Clint stared at her, then looked behind them.

"Okay," he said. "Let's get moving. You can tell me the rest on the way."

They started moving, and Rachel kept talking. Now that she'd started, she didn't seem able to stop. She told Clint her husband was abusive, physically and mentally, and that he and her father got along way too well.

"He gave my father money, and my brothers, and they enjoyed that. Even though they preferred to steal money rather than earn it, they didn't mind being given some."

"So what happened?"

"My husband died, suddenly," she said. "My father thinks I killed him."

"How did he die?"

"I don't know," she said. "He just . . . stopped breathing."

"Are you sure of that?"

"I'm positive," she said. "He was on top of me, at the time."

"I see . . . So you decided to . . . take the coffin to Austin, Texas, and . . ."

"And my father didn't like the idea of me leaving with it," she explained.

"So how did you?"

"I sneaked out at night," she said. "Caught the last boat downriver, and that's where you found me."

"So you're telling me your father is perfectly willing to kill people just to get you back?"

"Well . . . there is something else."

"And what's that?"

She turned her head to look at him when she answered, and he saw the tears in her eyes when she said, "I killed my younger brother, Billy, before I left."

"These tracks are real fresh, Dutch," Del Crockett said, looking down at the ruts left by the buckboard.

"How long?"

"A few hours, maybe."

"Boys," Dutch said, "let's move. We're gonna catch up to that bitch before nightfall."

Clint was fairly sure they'd never make it to Austin before the gunmen caught up to them.

"What if we kept moving while they camped?" Rachel asked.

"Traveling at night, we'd be risking the horses, or a wheel," he said, "or our necks. Besides, I think they'll catch up to us before nightfall." They were moving fairly quickly, but unencumbered by a buckboard, the riders should catch up to them with little or no problem.

"What can we do, then?"

"Well, one way to go would be for you to continue on, and for me to wait for them and pin them down."

"Wait where?"

"I'd have to find a likely spot pretty soon," he said. "They're only a few hours behind us, at best."

"How can you hold them off alone?" she asked.

"One man with a rifle can hold off a whole unit if he has a good enough vantage point."

"Like where?"

"High ground," he answered. "Top of a hill would do."

"Couldn't we both hold them off better with two rifles?" she asked him.

"I will have two rifles," Clint said. "Yours and mine."

"But—"

"If we're both holding them off," he asked, "the coffin and buckboard are not going to get to Austin by themselves."

She ducked her head sheepishly and said, "Oh."

"I'm going to ride ahead and see if I can find a good spot."

"Wait," she said, "you can't leave me—"

"I'm not going to go far," he promised, "but fire a shot if you need me."

Before she could protest again he urged his horse forward . . .

FIFTY-THREE

"Pa?"

"Yeah, Luke?"

"We ain't yet talked about what we're gonna do to Rachel when we catch up to her."

Dutch and Luke were riding ahead of the others. Behind them they could hear Coy and Sam arguing about something.

"Pa?"

"What, Luke?"

"Have you decided yet?"

Dutch turned his head and looked at Luke.

"She killed Billy, Luke. She killed your little brother." Dutch took a deep breath. "She killed her own brother!"

"Maybe it was an accident," Luke said. "We don't know what happened, Pa."

"We know what Billy said," Dutch replied. "He said Rachel shot him."

"I know Pa, but . . . we ain't heard Rachel's explanation."

"That's because she ran off," Dutch said. "She didn't stay to give us an explanation."

"Are you gonna listen to her? When we catch her, I mean?"

"I don't know."

"Pa . . . you ain't gonna kill 'er, are you?"

"I said I don't know what I'm gonna do, boy!" Dutch said.

"I'm still thinkin' on it. So just shut the hell up and let me think!"

An hour later Luke spoke again.

"Pa . . . I know Billy was the smartest of all of us, but—"

Dutch put his hand out to stop Luke from talking.

"Luke, you're the oldest and you're the smartest," he said. "You always was. But Billy . . . he was the best of us. He was gonna be somethin', and now, thanks to Rachel, that ain't ever gonna happen."

"I know, but—"

"And now you gotta shut up, because I'm still thinkin' about it. Get your brother Coy up here."

"Okay, Pa."

Luke rode back, got Coy and rode with him up alongside of Dutch.

"Coy, I want you to ride ahead and see what you can see."

"Okay, Pa," Coy said. "If I see them two, I'll—"

"You'll do nothin'," Dutch said. "If you see 'em, just come back and tell me how far ahead they are. That's all. You understand?"

"I understand, Pa."

"Okay, then. Go."

Coy kicked his horse in the ribs and rode ahead.

"Pa . . . why Coy? I coulda rode ahead and checked."

"That boy's gotta be good for somethin', Luke," Dutch said.

Luke had his doubts, but kept them to himself.

Coy rode up ahead, pushing his horse hard. When he thought he saw something, he slowed down. He didn't want to tip them off by making too much noise. He slowed his horse to a canter, and kept moving forward until he got a good clear look ahead. It was a buckboard, with a rider alongside.

"Gotcha," he said.

He thought about riding back and telling his pa, but instead decided to do something. He knew his father thought he was good for nothing, and this was his chance to prove him wrong, a chance to show that he actually had the brain, and the nerve, to be a Crater.

FIFTY-FOUR

Clint put his hand out to Rachel, waving at her to stop.

"What is it?" she asked.

He shushed her and listened for a moment before speaking.

"I have to ask you something, Rachel," he said.

"What?"

"These are your relatives," he said. "How are you going to feel if I have to kill some of them?"

"Clint," she said, "I don't care if you kill all of them."

"Rachel—"

"Remember, I killed my little brother, and my uncle."

He hadn't yet asked her how that had happened. What the circumstances were. It wasn't important as far as what he had to do. Maybe later, he'd find out the whole story, but it was sort of like whatever was in the coffin—he didn't have to know in order to act.

"All right," he said. "I think I heard something. I want you to just keep going and don't look back. If you hear shots, just keep on going."

"Clint—"

"I'll be along shortly."

"Are you going to do what you said? Pin them down?"

"Not yet," he said. "I may have something better."

"Like what?"

"I'll let you know." He dismounted, and tied his horse to

213

the side of the buckboard. "Keep going. I'll catch up on foot."

"Clint, how—"

But he had turned, and was gone.

The terrain was pretty flat. There were some hills here and there, but as far as cover there was very little available. Clint managed to find a stand of brush that would do the trick, if he crouched down real low. He did that, hoping he wasn't wrong, because the farther away Rachel got, the longer run he was going to have to catch up.

That's when he heard the horse.

Coy had his gun out already, in anticipation of catching up to Clint and his sister. In the end, that's what actually got him killed.

Clint stepped out from behind the brush and shouted, "Hold it there!"

Coy turned in his saddle at the sound of the voice, swinging his gun around with him. Clint saw the gun and felt he had no choice. He couldn't afford to wait and see what Coy had in mind.

He drew and fired.

Coy felt the fire burn into his chest, and his finger pulled the trigger of his gun convulsively, firing a round into the ground. He fell off his horse then, realizing—for the first time in his life—that he should have done exactly what his father had told him to do.

He was dead before he hit the ground.

Clint checked the body, after kicking the man's gun away from him, just in case. When he was satisfied that the man was dead, he wondered if this was one of Rachel's brothers. From what he could see, there was absolutely no family resemblance. Briefly, he wondered if Rachel's story about a father and brothers chasing her was even true.

He searched the body, looking for something with the man's name on it, but found nothing. Luckily, the man's horse had only cantered away a few feet. Clint gathered in the reins and went through the saddlebags. He found some beef jerky, and licorice, and an extra gun that needed cleaning, but still nothing to identify the man.

"Okay," he said to the horse, "I guess I'll just use you to catch up, and leave him right here for his friends—or family—to find."

He noticed that the brand on the horse was three-T's, which meant nothing to him. He mounted up, and stared down at the dead man for a long moment.

"If you hadn't had your gun out . . . ," he said, shaking his head. He might have been able to talk to the man, find out some things, but the way things stood now, he had to go along with Rachel's story. The tears he'd seen in her eyes when she told him she'd killed her own brother had seemed real enough, but on the other hand, she just finished telling him she didn't care if he killed her whole family.

The whole story was probably still somewhere in their future, but the present needed to be dealt with first. He was fairly sure she must have heard the shots, and that their pursuers must have heard them, as well. He looked at the sky. If their pursuers paused to bury this man, they wouldn't be able to catch up to him and Rachel before nightfall. Everybody might still have time to camp one more time.

As he started after Rachel, he hoped she was telling the truth and these men were related, because then they'd almost have to stop to bury their dead.

FIFTY-FIVE

Sheriff Carl Brody paused briefly to look down at the dead Dan Tanner and his men without dismounting.

"Sorry, boys," he said, "I don't have time to stop and bury you. Maybe on the way back."

But he knew that wouldn't be true. By the time he passed this way again, predators would have picked their bones clean. But there was no help for it. He had to move on.

Dutch and the others caught up to Coy after half an hour. Luke dismounted and checked his brother.

"He's dead, Pa," he said. "Drilled dead center."

Dutch stared down at his dead son.

"Stupid," he said. "He tried to take them himself."

"How do you know that?" Del asked.

"Because he's dead, damn it!"

"Pa—" Luke said.

"We'll have to bury him," Dutch said.

"If we do," Del said, "it'll get dark. We won't catch up to them tonight."

"Plenty of time tomorrow," Dutch said. "This is family. We've got to bury him."

"I could go on ahead," Del said. "Keep them in sight."

"You don't have to do that," Dutch said. "We'll catch up with them tomorrow."

Dutch dismounted, then looked at the others.

"Everybody digs."

Brody came upon them while they were digging what looked like a grave. He spotted the dead body and wondered what had happened. Had they fallen out among themselves? Or had one of them gone ahead and run into Clint Adams?

Brody looked around him. There wasn't much cover. In fact, if they turned around now, they'd see him. He couldn't sneak past them. But he could go around them if he rode wide enough. If he did that, he could catch up to Clint before they did. Together, he and Clint would be able to stand against them.

He wheeled his horse around and headed west. After a few hundred yards or so he'd head south again. It'd be dark soon. If Adams and the woman made camp, he'd be able to find them.

Rachel had heard the shots and was tempted to turn back. In fact she stopped, preparing to turn around, but then decided to just do what Clint had told her to do. He hadn't let her down, yet.

She continued on, heard no more shots, and eventually heard the horse behind her. When she turned, she saw it was Clint astride.

"What happened?"

He told her, and described the dead man to her.

"That'd be my brother Coy," she said. "He was the biggest, and dumbest, of the bunch."

"I'm sorry, Rachel," Clint said. "He didn't give me a choice."

"I told you I didn't care if you killed them," she said, "and I meant it, Clint."

"You cried when you talked about killing your younger brother, Billy."

She looked away and said, "There's a big difference between you killing my brother and me doing it."

FIFTY-SIX

Clint discussed the death of her brother Coy with Rachel.

"What will your father do?"

"He'll bury him," she said.

"No doubt?"

"None. Pa is very big on family—on sons," she amended. "He didn't think much of daughters."

"All right, then," Clint said. "It'll be dark by the time they finish. That means we can camp, rest the horses and make a run for Austin at first light."

"All right," she said. "That sounds okay with me."

Later, as he was building a fire, she asked, "Is that wise?"

"They know we're here," he said. "That's not a secret."

"Won't they try to take us in the dark?"

"They don't know the terrain, and neither do I," he said. "That's why I'm not planning on trying to find their camp. It's real easy to break a leg in country like this. I think we'd all rather face each other in the daylight."

"Pa would," she said. "He'll want to see me, see my eyes—and yours."

"We'll stand watch, anyway," Clint said, "as I'm sure they will."

Much the same conversation was talking place a few miles back.

219

"Pa, I can sneak up on them in the dark, I know I can," Sam said.

"That man will kill you, Sam," Dutch said, "without a second thought, just like he killed your uncle, and your brother. And that's if you don't kill yourself stumbling around in the dark. No, we'll wait until morning. We'll take them in the daylight."

"We'll stand watch, Pa," Luke said. "Sam, Del and me. You can get some sleep."

Dutch looked at his oldest son and said, "I'm gonna take you up on that offer, Luke."

Brody saw the light from the campfire and headed for it. He was on foot. Riding around in the dark, his horse had stepped in a chuck hole and fallen. The animal had broken its leg, and not wanting to fire a shot, Brody had to kill it by slitting its great throat. Now he was carrying his rifle and his saddlebags. He'd been unable to remove his saddle from the fallen animal.

He'd almost stepped in a hole himself, and once had stepped on a rock and turned his ankle, so now he was limping. If the others were all smart, they were bedded down and not stumbling around in the dark like he was.

Clint had taken the first watch, allowing the exhausted Rachel to bed down. It was quiet, so when the three horses—they'd decided to keep Coy's horse and had tied it to the back of the buckboard—got nervous, he knew that someone was approaching.

"Hello, the fire!" a man called.

Clint couldn't believe that one of Rachel's brothers would try something like this. The voice woke her.

"Who is it?" she hissed.

"I don't know," he answered. "Hello?" he called out. "Identify yourself."

"It's Sheriff Brody, from Oklahoma City," the voice said. "Is that you, Adams?"

"Come ahead, Sheriff," Clint said, holding his rifle ready. "Keep your hands where I can see them and come into the light."

"I'm on foot," Brody called back.

"Come ahead, then."

Clint and Rachel waited as the sheriff came slowly into view. Clint noticed that the lawman was limping and carrying his saddlebags.

"Come to the fire, Sheriff," he said, lowering the rifle. "You look like you could use a cup of coffee."

"And a meal," Rachel said, unfurling herself from her bedroll. "I'll fix you something."

"Much obliged for that, ma'am."

Brody approached the fire and sat down, setting his saddle-bags aside. Clint noticed dried blood on the man's arms.

"What happened to you horse?" he asked.

"Stepped in a chuck hole, broke his leg," Brody said. "I had to slit his throat in order to put him out of his misery quietly."

"That explains the dried blood on your arms," Clint said. "We can spare you some water to wash it off with."

"I appreciate that."

In fact, the canteen Clint passed to Brody had come off of Coy Crater's horse. The lawman poured some water over his arms, washing off the dried horse's blood.

"Here you go," Clint said, passing the man a cup of coffee.

"Thanks."

"Looks like your horse wasn't the only one to take a bad step," Clint observed.

Brody looked down at his right foot.

"Stepped on a rock, rolled my ankle some."

"Would you like to take off your boot so I can take a look?" Rachel asked.

"No thanks, ma'am," Brody said. "It's already swelled up, and if I take the boot off, I'll never get it back on again."

"Probably better to leave it on, then," Clint agreed.

The smell of bacon and beans filled the air as Rachel dropped some into the frying pan.

"You want to tell us what you're doing out here?" Clint asked.

"Did you know there was a posse out after you?" Brody asked.

"We knew somebody was on our trail."

"Two somebodies," Brody corrected. Briefly, he told Clint about Sergeant Tanner and his men, and then about the men who had killed the livery owner, and then the woman and her son, after which they'd burned down her ranch.

"Yesterday they caught up to the posse and wiped them out." He finished in time to accept a plate from Rachel.

"I know," Clint said. "I saw."

"You were watching, too?"

"Yes," Clint said, "but I didn't see you."

"I didn't see you, either," Brody said. "You the one that killed one of them, then?"

"Yeah," Clint said. "I doubled back and caught one of them trying to close in on us. Figured they'd take the time to bury their dead, giving us time to camp."

"You were right," Brody said. "I saw them digging a grave, so I went wide around them. Had to move in the dark, though, and it cost me my horse. Might have to hitch a ride with you on your buckboard."

"No need," Clint said. "We have the dead man's horse. It's yours."

"That's real generous of you."

"Least we can do, if you came all this way to help us," Clint said.

"Well, actually," the lawman said, "I'm tracking those killers. They just happen to be tracking you."

"Fair enough," Clint said. "The horse is still yours."

"Any idea why those men are tracking you?" Brody asked.

Clint looked at Rachel, then back at the lawman, and said, "We have some."

"It appears they arrived looking for those men you killed," Brody said. "I figured it was all connected."

"It's connected, all right."

After a moment of silence, Brody said, "Well, the whys and wherefores aren't any of my business, so I'm not gonna ask. However, there's four of them still back there, and they're likely to catch up to you tomorrow."

"You offering your help?" Clint asked.

"I'm proposing we join forces," Brody said.

"What are your intentions?"

"To arrest them and take them back to Oklahoma City."

Clint looked at Rachel, who simply stared back at him.

"That would suit us."

"So you're not intent on killing them?"

"I wasn't intent on killing that one yesterday," Clint said. "He had his gun out, and I had no choice."

"All right, then," Brody said. "I guess we'll need some kind of a plan." He finished the last of his food and handed the plate back to Rachel. "That was real fine, ma'am. Thank you."

"You're welcome," she said, "and stop calling me 'ma'am.' My name is Rachel."

"I could sure use some more of that coffee, Rachel."

She accepted his cup, refilled it and handed it back.

"Did you have some kind of plan in mind, Sheriff?" Clint asked.

"Nope," Brody said. "I thought you might."

"I had a couple of kicking around in my head."

"Well, let's hear 'em," Brody said. "Maybe I can add something that might be helpful."

"Maybe you can," Clint said.

"Mind if I sit in on this?" Rachel asked.

"Why not?" Clint said. "You got more invested than any of us."

They put their heads together over some more coffee and tried to hash out a plan.

FIFTY-SEVEN

Rachel went back to her bedroll while Clint and Brody were still discussing possible plans.

"Can I ask you something?" Brody said while they were waiting for another cup of coffee.

"Sure, why not?"

"What's in the coffin?"

"She says it's her husband."

"In this heat?" Brody asked. "I'd be able to smell him from here—plus, he probably would have bloated up by now and"—he looked over at Rachel to see if she was listening—"and burst through the wood."

"To tell you the truth," Clint said, "I don't know what's in the coffin."

"Aren't you curious?"

"I was, but not anymore."

"Why not?"

"Because I'm getting paid to transport her and the coffin to Austin, safely," Clint said. "That's all I care about."

Brody looked over at the buckboard, then back across the fire at Clint.

"I gotta tell you, I'd have looked by now."

Clint poured the lawman another cup of coffee, and the man settled back into a more comfortable position.

"You're a better man than I am."

"How so?" Clint asked.

"I would have snuck a look by now, like I said."

Clint hesitated, then said, "I can't say the thought never entered my mind."

"Ah," Brody said, "a crack."

"Crack?"

"In the legend."

Clint didn't reply.

"I'm sorry," Brody said. "I was just kidding. I didn't mean any offense. It's just . . . I couldn't be that removed."

"It comes with practice."

"She must be paying you a lot of money to haul this dead weight to hell and gone."

Clint stared at Brody.

"Oh, hey," Brody said, "don't get me wrong. I don't begrudge you making a living. And I'm not interested in anything but doing my job. It's just that . . . I'm naturally curious."

"I guess you'll have to ask Rachel, then," Clint said. "Maybe she'll tell you."

"You're right," Brody said. "Maybe she will."

"So just doing your job," Clint said, "that brings you all the way out here?"

"Okay, so it's a little more than that," Brody said, without hesitation. "I knew the people these animals killed. Ray Toller was just trying to make a living. Gayle Truscott and her son were just trying to survive."

"I see."

"No, it wasn't like that," Brody said. "Sure, I knew Gayle, but not that well. I just felt sorry for her after her husband died, and I admired her for trying to go on. These animals cut her life short just when it might have started going good for her and the boy. He was only twelve."

Clint looked at Brody, then at the sleeping Rachel.

"They're her family."

"What?"

"Her father, brothers," Clint said. "The one I killed yesterday was a brother."

"How does she feel about that?"

"Says she doesn't care," Clint said. "In fact, they're after her because she killed her younger brother herself."

Brody blinked and was speechless for a moment.

"Wow!" he finally said. "She tell you all this?"

"Yeah."

"You believe her?"

"Not completely."

"Wouldn't showing you what's in the coffin go a long way toward helping you to believe her?"

"No," Clint said, "paying me would do that."

"Mind if I ask how much she's supposed to pay you?"

"There goes that curiosity again."

"Sorry."

Brody leaned forward, and made the fire flare by tossing the remnants of his coffee into it.

"I can take the first watch," he said. "My foot's throbbing. I wouldn't be able to sleep, anyway."

"You going to be able to get around on it tomorrow?"

"As long as I'm riding more than I'm walking."

"Okay, then," Clint said. "Wake me in a few hours."

"Sure."

Clint went to his bedroll, but given the nature of some of the questions the lawman had asked, he didn't think he'd be getting much sleep.

FIFTY-EIGHT

Dutch Crater was sitting by the fire, holding in his hand the sergeant's badge they'd taken off one of the dead men.

"Pa?"

Dutch looked up and saw Luke.

"You okay, Pa?"

"I thinkin', Luke," Dutch said. "Just thinkin'."

"About what?"

"Austin," Dutch said. "I'm thinkin' about lettin' Rachel and her gunfighter make it to Austin."

"Why would we do that, Pa?"

"Because your cousin Floyd will be there, with some men," the older man replied.

"Yeah, but, we can get 'em out in the open tomorrow—"

"Luke," Dutch said, "we don't know who Rachel has with her, but we know that he's killed a whole passel of men, including your brother Coy. He's gotta be pretty damn good to do that."

"There's four of us, Pa," Luke said, "and one of him. Coy was stupid enough to try to go up against him by hisself, but—"

"You're forgettin' somethin'."

"What?"

"Your sister can shoot, too."

229

"Rachel?" Luke looked confused. "You think she'd shoot at us?"

"Luke, she killed Billy."

"I ain't so sure about that—"

Dutch reached out and grabbed Luke's left arm in a painful grip.

"He told me so!" he hissed. "You think your brother lied to me on his deathbed?"

"No, but—"

Dutch released Luke's arm, stared back down at the badge in his hand.

"I'm thinkin' we got these badges to hide behind once we get to Austin," Dutch said. "We can use 'em to deal with the local law if we come up against 'em. Meanwhile, we meet up with Floyd and his men, and then we got enough guns to take this fella."

"Pa," Luke said, "we can take him, I know we can."

Dutch looked at Luke, and the younger man saw something in his father's eyes he'd never seen before—pain.

"I ain't gonna risk another one of my boys," he said. "It's bad enough I gotta kill my own daughter when I catch up to her; I ain't gonna lose another one of my sons to do it."

The impact of what Dutch had just said hit Luke Crater hard, and he blinked.

"Pa," he said, "you ain't decided to kill Rachel, have you?"

Luke was still staring into his father's eyes when something suddenly changed there and Dutch said, "Oh, yeah."

FIFTY-NINE

Sheriff Brody kept watch while Clint and Rachel broke camp and got the horses ready, just in case the Crater bunch appeared on the horizon before they were ready to move.

"Maybe I should stay behind," Brody suggested, when they were ready to move on. "Keep them pinned down so you can make Austin."

Clint and Rachel exchanged a glance, because they had talked about such a plan before Brody arrived.

"If we're going to do that," Clint said, "we have to find a better spot than this for it. Let's ride for a while. We probably have a few hours on them."

"Okay."

They considered letting Brody drive the buckboard because of his bad foot, but in the end he decided that he'd be much more comfortable on horseback.

They moved out with Clint riding alongside of Rachel and Brody bringing up the rear, keeping an eye out behind them.

"You didn't sleep much last night," Rachel said to Clint.

Clint leaned over toward her. "Let's just say I'm not completely sold on Brody."

"You didn't tell him how much I was paying you, did you?" she asked.

"No," Clint said, "but he's got his curiosity about that coffin."

"What did you tell him was in it?"

"I told him what you told me," Clint said. "He drew his own conclusions from that."

"I feel kind of sorry for you, Clint."

"Why's that?"

"Well, you haven't trusted me completely from the start, and now you don't trust the sheriff. That's got to be a lonely feeling."

"I'm getting paid for it," he told her.

The Craters broke camp, and Dutch told Del and Sam what he had discussed last night with Luke.

"What do you think?" he asked.

"You're the boss, Dutch," Del said. "I'll go along with whatever you say."

"Me, too," Sam chimed in.

"Del, I need you to do somethin' for me, and I need you to do it to the letter, understand?"

"Sure, Dutch."

"Okay," Dutch said. "Ride on ahead and spot them for me. That's all. Don't let 'em see you, and don't try to take them. Just come back and let me know how far ahead they are. You got me, boy?"

"I got you, Dutch," Del said. "Don't worry. I'll be back."

"Good boy."

Del mounted up and rode ahead.

"Pa, why'd you send Del ahead?" Luke asked. "I coulda went."

"You're my son," Dutch said, simply. "He's not."

Del rode full-out for a short time, then slowed his horse to a canter. He didn't want to end up riding up on Rachel and her gunman too fast. Apparently, Coy had encountered them when he wasn't ready, and look what had happened to him.

While he rode, Del thought about Rachel. He'd been in love with her ever since they were kids. For a while, during their early teens, he thought she felt the same way, but then he fell under Dutch's sway, and she began to look at him with the same eyes that saw her father and brothers, and she didn't like what she saw. Del had never been able to figure out what went wrong, and even now he hoped that things would change—if Dutch didn't kill her first.

Brody rode up alongside Clint after a couple of hours.

"Seems to me they could have caught up to us by now."

"I was thinking the same thing, Sheriff," Clint said. "But maybe they don't want to."

"Why wouldn't they?"

"The odds are different," Clint said. "There were five of them, right? And they didn't lose any men when they took that posse."

"Right."

"And they thought they were just tracking Rachel and me," he went on. "Now you're here, and they lost a man."

"It's still two against four," Brody said.

"Three," Clint said. "Three against four. Rachel can shoot."

"But . . . they're her family."

"And she doesn't care about that."

"But how would they know about me?"

"I think we have to assume they've scouted us by now."

Sheriff Brody turned his head to look around before he could catch himself.

"So . . . why would they let us get to Austin?"

"The only thing I can think of is, they probably have help waiting there."

"Well then," Brody said, "maybe we should force a confrontation."

"Yeah, maybe," Clint said, "but we still might be better off making it to Austin before that."

"Well," Brody said, "I guess if they're not going to try to take us out in the open, we have time to decide."

"Having more time," Clint said, "doesn't always lead to the right decision."

Dutch saw Del riding back and stopped to wait for him. He was surprised at how relieved he as to see the young man returning safely, even though Del wasn't one of his sons.

"Dutch."

"Where are they?"

"About two hours ahead," Del said, "but there's three of them."

"What?" Dutch said. "Who's with them?"

"I couldn't tell, so I circled around and caught the sun flashing off something on the other man's chest."

"A lawman?"

"Looks like it."

"So there's three of them," Dutch said. "Well, that cinches it. Boys, we're just gonna trail behind them and wait until they get to Austin before we hit them."

"Pa," Sam said.

"What, Sam?"

"Why don't we just go around them," Sam asked, "and get to Austin first?"

Dutch, Luke and Del all turned their heads to look at Sam. Maybe, Dutch thought, there was some hope for Sam yet.

Clint and Brody finally decided that the lawman should ride back and check on the location of Dutch Crater and his boys.

"Don't do anything foolish," Clint said to Brody. "Just take a look and get right back here."

"Gotcha," Brody said.

"And I suggest you take off that badge," Clint said. "It'll reflect the sun."

"Good thinking."

Brody took the badge off, put it in his pocket, then turned his horse and rode off.

"Now we're trusting him?" Rachel asked.

"This far, yeah," Clint said. "He really is a lawman, and there's no reason to think he has any connection with your family . . . is there?"

"Not that I can see."

"Then let's keep going,"

Brody was confused.

He'd ridden back far enough to come within sight of their pursuers, only there were no pursuers. Was it possible they'd turned back? That the death of one of their number had changed their minds?

He rode back a little farther, until he was absolutely certain they were not there, and then turned and headed back to Clint and Rachel.

Clint turned at the sound of Brody's horse. Rachel reined her horse in and turned in her seat.

"He's in a hurry," she said.

Clint nodded. When Brody reached them, he reined his horse in and faced them with a confused look on his face.

"They're not there."

"What?" Rachel asked.

"I rode back further than I should have," Brody said. "They're not there. They turned back."

"They gave up?" Rachel asked. She looked at Clint. "That's not likely, Clint."

"No, it isn't," Clint said. "There's something else that's more likely."

"What's that?" Brody asked.

Clint turned and looked south.

"They circled us and went ahead."

"They're going to ambush us along the trail?" Rachel asked.

"No," Clint said, "I mean, they went ahead." He looked at the two of them. "They're going to be waiting for us in Austin."

SIXTY

They rode into Austin, drawing no attention for the fact that they had a coffin with them. The city was so busy no one was paying them any attention at all—that they could tell.

"Where do we go?" Clint asked Rachel.

"Why are you asking me?"

"You're the one who wanted to get to Austin," he reminded her. "You're here."

"But I've never been here before," she said. "I don't know where to go."

"Well," Clint said, "we could find the nearest undertaker."

She gave him a look that said, *You know there's not really a body in that box, don't you?*

"Or a hotel," he added.

"That sounds good to me," she said. "A real bath and some clean clothes and I might start to feel human again."

"What are you going to do with the coffin?" Brody asked.

"We'll leave it on the buckboard, stick the whole thing in a livery," Clint said. "What about you? What are your plans?"

"I think I'll wait and see what hotel you end up in, and then I'll go check in with the local law."

"Maybe we should find the train station," Rachel suggested.

"Why?"

"So we can stay away from it."

They continued down the street until they found a hotel large enough to have its own livery.

"We'll be here," Clint told Brody as they stopped in front of the Congress Hotel.

"I'll find the local law, let them know what's going on," Brody said. "See you back here."

Clint nodded. Brody continued on while Clint helped Rachel down from the buckboard. Now that they had stopped, people were finding the presence of a coffin in the back of the buckboard interesting.

They entered the hotel and crossed the large lobby to the front desk. The fact that they were covered with trail dust was enough to attract attention there.

"We need two rooms, please," Clint said.

"Of course, sir," the middle-aged clerk said. "You have, uh, funds?"

"We can pay," Rachel said. She took some money from her pocket to show the man.

"Very well, then," he said, turning the register around for them to sign in. "One room?"

"That'll be fi—" Rachel started, but Clint cut her off.

"Two," Clint reminded him.

"Of course, sir. Adjoining?"

"Not necessarily."

"Yes, sir," the man said, He turned and retrieved two keys. "Five and six, sir, across the hall from each other."

"Fine."

"Do you have luggage?"

Rachel looked at Clint, and Clint said to the man, "Kind of . . ."

After he'd explained about the buckboard and coffin, the clerk decided there was no problem putting both in the livery.

"I can have it done for you, if you like—"

"No," Clint said, "I'll drive it in myself." He turned to Rachel. "You got to your room, have your bath. I'll see you in a little while."

"Where should we meet?"

"I'll come to your room."

"The sooner the better," she said. Then: "Oh, there's one more thing." She turned to the clerk. "Where's the railway station?"

"Not very far from here, actually," the man said. "Austin is the westernmost station of the Houston and Texas Central Railway. Do you want to go to the station?"

"No," Rachel said, "actually, we want to stay away from there."

SIXTY-ONE

Clint got the buckboard and coffin situated, and then went back into the hotel, to his room. It never occurred to him to get a look inside the coffin. The only thing he thought he knew for sure was that there definitely wasn't a body in there. Whatever was in there, then, was Rachel's business—especially since they'd made it safely to Austin. He knew what he should have done now was make her pay him and be on his way, except that her demented family was somewhere in Austin.

He carried his saddlebags to his room. He didn't have time for a bath, so he used the pitcher and basin in the room to clean up as well as he could, then pulled his last clean shirt—the one Rachel had washed on the trail—from his saddlebags and put it on. He walked across the hall and knocked on Rachel's door.

"Come in."

He entered and found her naked, in a bathtub.

"This is great," she said. "I had them fill it for me as hot as I could stand it, and it's still hot."

"It's time for me to get paid," he said.

"Is it?"

"Yes."

"And then what?" she asked. "Will you be leaving?"

"Not while your . . . father and brothers are around," he said.

241

"Are you worried about me, Clint?"

"What's the point of me getting you here," he asked, "if they're just going to kill you?"

"And you wouldn't want me to get killed before I pay you, right?" she asked.

"Right. So, do we have to go to the bank to get the money?"

"No," she said, standing up, "we don't."

He watched as the water sluiced off her body, over her heavy breasts, dripping from her swollen nipples, and down her belly.

She stepped from the tub and approached him, reached down between his legs.

"First things first," she said.

When Dutch and his boys had arrived in Austin earlier that day, they'd gone directly to the railroad station. There, they'd found Cousin Floyd Crater waiting with two men.

"Two men?" Dutch complained. "That's all you brought?"

"You sent me a telegram tellin' me to watch for your daughter, Rachel," Floyd said. "I thought two men might be too much."

"Well, she's got two men with her now," Dutch said. "A gunman and a lawman. We're gonna need more men."

"Where are the rest of your boys?" Floyd asked. He pointed at Del. "He don't look like a Crater, but them two do."

"That's Del Crockett," Dutch said. "These are my boys Luke and Sam."

"Didn't you have four boys?"

Dutch glared at Floyd and said, "That's right, I did."

Brody checked in with the local sheriff, who promised every cooperation.

"As soon as you locate them boys," Sheriff Ed Peters said, "you let me know." He was in his mid-fifties, and had been sheriff of Austin for a long time.

"Do you have a police department here?" Brody asked.

"We do," Peters said, making a face. "They wear these fancy blue uniforms. Gettin' too damn modern out here, but between you and me, it's us sheriffs who are still the real law in the West."

"Not for long, I'm afraid," Brody said. "I suppose I should check in with them, as well."

"That's up to you," Peters said, "but I got enough deputies to back your play. Just who is it you're lookin' for?"

Brody thought for a moment, then dredged up the name Clint had given him.

"You know a family named Crater?"

"Crater?" Sheriff Peters asked. "Maybe I don't have enough deputies . . ."

She tried to pull him into the bathtub with her, but he said they'd already made love in water. He wanted to use a bed. She did, however, manage to get his clothes wet before they got them off and hit the bed.

He was again amazed at how bountiful her charms were, and how they did not seem so when she was dressed. He spent a lot of time on her breasts, now that they were not on the trail. She held the back of his head while he kissed them, licked them, bit the rigid nipples until she squirmed and moaned.

"My turn," she said, abruptly changing their positions so that he was on his back and she was on top.

She kissed his chest, his belly, worked her way down to his erect penis, where she returned the favor and spent much time kissing, licking and touching. He kept waiting for her to take him in her mouth, but she seemed happy enough to tease him to the point of bursting, and then back off. Before long it was he who was doing the squirming, and before she drove him out of his mind, he decided to change their positions again.

He flipped her onto her back, then asserted himself again by abruptly turning her over onto her stomach. He kneaded her almost chunky buttocks, then leaned over and bit them, pausing to run his tongue along the crease between them. She wiggled her butt in his face with a sigh, and he slid one hand beneath her so he could slide one finger over her moist slit while still massaging her ass with the other.

"Oh, my," she said, grinding herself down onto his finger.

Moving again, he got behind her, pulled her up onto all

fours, then slid his rock-hard cock up between her smooth thighs and into her. She gasped as he took hold of her hips and began pounding in and out of her like that, from behind. She got into the rhythm with him, slamming her ass back against him each time he thrust forward. At one point he thought her gasps and cries were interrupted by a snort. They both started to sweat with the exertion, and as they both neared their completion, he reached out to pull her up onto her knees and against him so he could turn her head and kiss her. Her breath was hot on his mouth, her tongue acid in his mouth, and then he pushed her back down, grabbed her by the hair and rode her that way until they were both finished . . .

"Do you have any family in Austin, Rachel?" he asked. "That you know of?" He was sitting on the bed, pulling his boots back on. Next and last would be his gunbelt, which was on the bedpost.

"The Craters have family all over the country," she said. "It's possible."

"Uncle Roy was in Oklahoma City," he reminded her. "You can't recall any family being mentioned here in Austin?"

She thought a moment, then said, "Sorry."

"All right," he said. "Get dressed."

"Where are we going?" she asked, rolling over and propping herself up on one elbow. "Out to dinner?"

"Sure," he said, "but first we're going to get my money."

"You have a one-track mind, Clint Adams, don't you?" she asked, scowling at him.

"Well, you may have derailed it for a while," he said, standing up, "but it's back on course now."

SIXTY-TWO

When Clint and Rachel came down to the lobby, they found Sheriff Brody waiting, seated on a divan.

"Didn't you get a room?" Clint asked him.

"I can't afford a place like this."

"Oh, I'm so sorry," Rachel said. "Let me get you a room right now."

"No, no," Brody said. "I found a place I could afford and, frankly, I prefer it to this. But you can buy me dinner."

"Just what we intended to do," Rachel said. "All right if we eat here?"

"Fine with me."

They went into the dining room, were seated and ordered their dinner right away. All three realized how hungry they truly were.

"Did you talk to the law?"

"I talked to the sheriff here, fella named Peters," Brody said. "I decided I'd prefer that to talking to the Austin Police Department."

"Well," Clint said, "after what we went through with the Oklahoma City Police Department . . ."

"Exactly," Brody said.

"Did you tell him our situation?"

"I did, and at first he promised cooperation," Brody said. "He said he had enough deputies to help us out."

"You said, 'at first'?" Rachel asked.

"Yeah," Brody said. "He changed his mind after I told him the man we were after were named Crater."

"And why's that?"

"He mentioned a Floyd Crater?"

"Jesus," Rachel said. "Cousin Floyd. I forgot about him."

"Well, apparently he's pretty well known around here," Brody said. "According to Peters, Floyd can put his hands on twenty or so guns at a moment's notice and most of them would be related to him."

Clint looked at Rachel.

"I knew Dutch had relatives all over," she said, "but I had no idea he had so many in Texas."

"So what did the sheriff say?"

"He suggested I talk to the police department after all," Brody said. "I'll have to do that in the morning."

"We'll just have to be on our toes until then," Clint said.

The waiter came with their dinners, and they gave up their conversation for a while in order to satisfy their hunger.

In another part of the city Dutch Crater was eating a steak in a small café that was more to his liking than many of the other eating establishments he had come across. He didn't like Austin, and wanted to finish their business and leave as soon as possible.

The café was on a side street, and was small and unpopular. It had no name, and was quite dirty, which didn't bother Dutch at all. It didn't bother his boys, either. The only member of his family who had a problem with dirt was his daughter, Rachel. She had always thought she was better than her family, and marrying a man with money had been her way of getting away from them, only it hadn't worked. The rich man she picked had turned out to be more like her pa than she knew.

Now her way of getting away from her family had been fleeing from Alton—and Missouri—in the dead of night, taking everything she valued with her. When her brother Billy had tried to stop her, she'd shot him in the belly and left him to die.

Dutch ordered another beer and had just received it when Luke, Del and Sam walked in.

"Anything?" Luke asked, sitting opposite his father.

"No," Dutch said. "I ain't heard nothing from Floyd."

"You wouldn't think it would be so hard to find a buck-board with a coffin on it," Del said.

"It's this place," Dutch said, meaning Austin. "It's too big."

"Too uppity," Sam said.

"That, too."

Austin had recently solidified itself as the capital of Texas, and was also the home of Texas's first university. It was just not a place for anyone named Crater to live.

"Get yerselves somethin' ta eat," Dutch said. He looked around, and the place was empty except for him and his boys. "Before the rush starts."

"How come nobody eats here?" Sam asked. "It looks okay to me."

"Wait till you taste the food," Dutch said. "But the price is right, and you don't have to wear a tie or take a bath before they serve you."

They called the waiter over and all ordered steak dinners. The waiter—also the owner—was thankful, because he was having his best day in weeks.

"And onions," Luke called out, as the waiter headed for the kitchen, where he turned into the cook. "Lots of onions."

"Not on mine!" Sam called. He looked around the table, smiled and said, "I might wanna get me a whore later. Don't wanna be breathin' onions into the poor darlin's face."

"You're real considerate," Del said.

"Nobody's gettin' no whores," Dutch said, although he intended to have one himself, later. "The only whore we're worried about right now is your sister."

"Guess it wasn't such a good idea to get here ahead of her, huh, Pa?" Luke asked.

"Hey." Sam wanted to defend the only good idea he'd ever had. "Who knew this place was so big and fancy?"

"Don't worry," Dutch said. "Floyd will find her. He's got the town covered."

"What about the law?" Luke asked.

"He's got that covered, too."

At that moment, as if right on cue, Floyd appeared at the door. He came over and joined them. Even to Dutch and his boys—who were Craters through and through—Floyd's body odor was hard to take in an enclosed space.

"Whataya got, Floyd?" Dutch asked.

"I found 'er," he said.

"Good," Del said. "Where is she?" The faster they found out, the faster he'd leave. Del didn't want to have to try to actually swallow food with Floyd around.

"Hotel called the Congress," Floyd said.

"Fancy place?" Dutch asked.

"The fanciest," Floyd said. "Got bathtubs in the rooms, and their own stable."

"Figures," Dutch said.

"She always thought she was better'n us, Pa," Sam said.

"Shut up," Dutch said.

"The coffin is still on the buckboard, in the hotel's stable," Floyd said.

"Okay," Dutch said. "How many men you got?"

"Five, countin' me."

"That makes . . . ," Sam said, then had trouble finishing because of the math.

"Nine of us," Del said.

Sam gave him a hard look. "I woulda got it."

"We ain't got all night," Luke said.

"Okay, Floyd," Dutch said. "Thanks."

"When do we move?" Floyd asked.

"Tomorrow," Dutch said. "Meet us here with your men in the morning, around nine."

"Here?" Floyd looked around.

"What's wrong with here?"

"It's filthy," Floyd said, "and the food's bad."

"The price is right," Dutch said. "Besides, who're you to talk about someplace bein' filthy." Dutch reached out and tapped his cousin's sleeve, sending up a little puff of dust.

"Hey," he said, "this is my best shirt."

"Well, do me a favor," Dutch said, "tomorrow, wear your second-best shirt."

After Floyd left and the others were eating their meals, Dutch played back that comment in his head and thought, Jesus, maybe that's where Rachel got her clean streak from.

SIXTY-THREE

"I think," Carl Brody said around bites of pie, "we'd be better off not counting on the local law for help."

"Why not?" Rachel asked, a confused look on her face. "Isn't that their job?"

"It's just that we won't be disappointed that way," Clint explained to her.

"Oh."

"I'll talk to the chief of police tomorrow, but I don't hold out much hope. I'm just an old-fashioned sheriff," he explained, "and I'm not even a Texas sheriff."

"I understand," Clint said.

"How long are you going to stay in Austin, Clint?" Brody asked. "I mean, after you get paid."

"Don't worry, Sheriff," Clint said. "I'm not going to run out on you. I told you I'd help you get these men, and I will."

"By the way," Rachel asked. "How's your foot?"

"Oh, I meant to tell you," Brody said. "I found myself walking—well, limping—past a doctor's office, so I went in. Turns out it ain't so bad. The swelling went down some. I was even able to get my boot back on after he took it off."

"That's good," she said.

"Yeah," Brody said, "a gimpy man wearing a badge is a target."

Rachel finished the last hunk of her pie and then sat back in her chair.

"I'm stuffed," she said.

"So am I," Brody said.

"I think I'm going to go back to my room," she said.

"Clint," Brody asked, "you want to get a beer in the bar?"

"Well," Clint said, "Rachel and I were going to finish up some business—"

"We can do that tomorrow, Clint," she said. "I'm really very tired from our trip, and that hot bath I had took a lot out of me." She gave Clint a meaningful look he hoped Brody had missed.

"All right, then," Clint said. "Tomorrow."

They paid their bill, and then the two men walked Rachel out to the lobby.

"Good night to both of you," she said. "Don't get too drunk tonight. I have a feeling we have a big day tomorrow."

"Don't worry," Clint said. "We'll turn in early."

"Sorry," she said, touching Clint's arm, "that's what comes from growing up with brothers."

She nodded to both of them and then went to her room.

Clint and Brody crossed the lobby and entered the hotel bar. They ordered a beer each and then went to a table. They had their pick, since there were only a few tables being used.

"Not many people," Brody observed.

"No gambling," Clint said, "no girls. Just a simple hotel bar. The only men coming in here are those who just want a drink, and conversation."

"That explains it." Brody took a sip of his beer. "I thought Rachel was unhappy with her family?"

"She is."

"That comment about growing up with brothers," Brody said. "It didn't sound like someone unhappy with their up-bringing."

"Maybe it wasn't all unhappy," Clint said.

"I suppose," Brody said. "My childhood had its moments . . . didn't yours?"

Clint responded by drinking his beer.

Brody figured he wasn't going to get anything personal out of Clint, so he decided to discuss business instead.

"I need your advice."

"On what?" Clint asked.

"Austin's a big town," Brody said. "Unless the police can tell me exactly where to find Floyd Crater, I'm going to have to wander around town looking for him."

"Or?"

"Or . . . That's what I was going to ask you," Brody said.

"Well, the alternative I see," Clint said, "is to wait for them to come to us."

"You think they can find us any easier than we can find them?" Brody asked.

"We're looking for some men," Clint said. "They're looking for a buckboard with a coffin on the back—and they have someone who lives here to help them. So, to answer your question . . . yes."

SIXTY-FOUR

Before going back to her room, Rachel went to the livery and did what she had to do without being seen. She checked the lobby on the way back, to be sure Clint and Brody were not there, then hurried to the stairs and up to her room.

Clint went right back to his room from the hotel bar, deciding not to drop in on Rachel again. When he woke up the next morning, he decided to get his money from her first thing, before they did anything else. He got washed, dressed and crossed the hall to her room. She answered his knock right away, but gave him an unhappy look.

"I thought you might come by last night."

"I thought we could all use some rest," he said.

"You're probably right. Time for breakfast?" She started to step out into the hall and close her door.

"We have some business first, Rachel," he said, using his foot to stop the door.

"But . . . aren't you hungry?"

"I can wait a few more minutes," he said. "Shouldn't take longer than that to count out five thousand dollars."

"This is your mercenary side, isn't it?" she asked.

"I just want what's coming to me."

"How do I know you won't just leave once you have your money?" she asked.

253

He grinned and said, "You know."

She tried to match his stare for a moment, then rolled her eyes and said, "Yeah, damn you, you're right. I do."

She backed into the room, and he followed, closing the door behind them. She walked to the chest of drawers by the window, took an envelope from the top drawer and handed it to him. Inside was five thousand dollars.

"How about breakfast now?" he asked.

"Let's go," she said. "You're buying."

Dutch arrived at the café first and ordered a pot of coffee and nine cups.

"That's gonna take two pots," the waiter said.

"Bring 'em then."

By the time the others arrived—Luke first, with Del and Sam in tow, and then Floyd and his men—Dutch had both pots on the table. As they entered, he filled all nine cups.

"Drink up," he said. "This is all the breakfast you'll get until we're finished."

Floyd picked up a cup and said, "We have to talk. Alone."

Dutch picked up a cup and said, "Step into my office." They moved to a back table, away from the others.

"What's wrong?" Dutch asked.

"These fellas have to get paid," Floyd said. "They ain't family."

"They won't do it for you?"

"Risk their lives?" Floyd asked. "Not hardly."

"What makes them think they'll be riskin' their lives?" Dutch asked.

"Clint Adams."

"You tell them that?"

"They got a right to know . . ."

"Tell them they'll get a thousand dollars each if they kill him."

"A thousand?" Floyd's surprise was obvious. "You got that much money?"

"Rachel does," Dutch said. "All we have to do is take it away from her."

"What's the problem with her, anyway?"

"She's not exactly happy with her family," Dutch said, "and we're not happy with her."

"Do they have to . . . make sure she doesn't get hurt?" Floyd asked his cousin.

"No," Dutch said, shaking his head. "They can to do whatever they have to do."

Floyd thought a moment, then said, "We can get them for five hundred each."

"Then the rest is yours," Dutch said.

Floyd smiled, revealing yellowed teeth, and said, "That's what I was thinkin'."

"Then drink your coffee," Dutch said, "and let's go."

SIXTY-FIVE

Brody had to wait an hour to get in to see the chief of police. It didn't surprise him. As soon as the policeman on the front desk saw his Oklahoma City sheriff's badge, he knew he'd have to wait. Finally, though, he was shown into the man's office and explained the situation to him.

"Do you have any posters on these men?" Chief Henry Clay asked him.

"No, sir," Brody said. "There wasn't time. I started tracking them after they killed Ray Toller, and discovered the bodies of Gayle Truscott and her son on my way."

"And this other man? Clint Adams? He's already in Austin?"

"Yes, sir."

Brody fell into calling the chief "sir," because of the man's age. He was at last sixty, with a head of shocking white hair. In fact, the man reminded Brody of his late father. But the resemblance ended with the physical.

"Sheriff," the man said, "you don't mind if I send a telegram to the Oklahoma City Police Department, do you?"

"No, sir," Brody said, "but you better tell them that I also discovered the bodies of five of their men, including Sergeant Dan Tanner."

"We'll get this cleared up as quickly as possible, sir," the chief said.

257

"I hope so," Brody said. "Two people's lives may depend on it."

Clint and Rachel were having breakfast—once again in the hotel dining room, for the sake of convenience—when they heard some commotion out in the lobby of the hotel.

"What's going on?" Clint asked a passing waiter.

"There are some policemen causing a disturbance in the lobby."

"Policemen?"

"Yes," the waiter said, "and they're not even from here, they're from Oklahoma City—and they smell terrible!"

Clint and Rachel exchanged a look. He was wearing his gun, and so was she, but all they had between them were the two handguns.

"Do you think—" she asked.

"Just sit tight and let me check."

He got up and walked to the door.

Dutch had instructed Floyd to have two of his men wait out front, and two to go around to the livery stable.

"I've got five Oklahoma City Police badges," he told his cousin. "You, me and the boys are gonna wear 'em when we go inside."

"Sounds like fun," Floyd had said; then he noticed Dutch was wearing a sergeant's badge.

"How come you get to be a sergeant?" he demanded.

"Only got one sergeant's badge, Floyd," Dutch said. "You wanna fight me for it now?"

Floyd had given in, and they entered the lobby . . .

When Clint looked out the door and across the lobby, he saw five grubby, dirty men wearing badges, talking to the clerk. This was stupid, he thought. He didn't even know what the Craters looked like. He turned and waved at Rachel to join them. Other diners in the room were staring at them.

"Is that them?" he asked her, when she'd joined him.

"Yeah," she said, "that's them."

"There's five of 'em," Clint said.

"One must be Cousin Floyd."

"There must be more somewhere," Clint said. "If you father wanted to take us with five men, he could have done it on the trail. The point of coming here was to have more men."

Suddenly Clint saw the clerk point toward the dining room.

"We've got to get out of here, now!" Clint said. "We're outgunned."

"But where do we go?"

"Through the kitchen," Clint said. "Maybe there's a way to the livery."

"The livery?"

"We need more guns, Rachel," he said.

"I think I know where we can get them," she said.

He looked at her and asked, "In the coffin?"

"In the coffin."

Dutch finally scared the clerk into pointing the way to the dining room.

"They're in there?"

"Y-yessir," the frightened man said. "I s-saw them go in just a little while ago."

Dutch turned and said to his boys, "Come on," and led the way across the lobby, shoving people out of his way.

When they got to the dining room, they burst in and looked around. Many of the tables were taken, but Dutch didn't see Rachel anywhere. A waiter started to pass with a tray of food, and Dutch grabbed him. The plates went flying all over, showering several diners with steak and eggs.

"Hey—" one man shouted.

Floyd stepped over and beat the man with his pistol. The woman seated with him screamed.

"You got anything else to say?" Floyd demanded.

The man, bleeding from the head, said, "Quiet, Martha."

"We're lookin' for a man and a woman," Dutch announced loudly, still holding the waiter by the front of the shirt. "If we find 'em, nobody else gets hurt."

Nobody spoke for a moment, then the waiter said, "A man and a woman w-went into the kitchen."

"Where can they get to from there?" Dutch demanded.

"The back of the hotel," the frightened waiter said, "and the livery stable."

"We got the stable covered, Pa!" Luke said.

"Yeah," Dutch said, releasing the waiter and flinging him across the room, "let's go. We got 'em!"

Clint and Rachel went into the kitchen and asked one of the cooks for the back door.

"There!" the man said, pointing.

"Can we get to the stable from there?"

"Yeah," the man said, "go to the left, you'll get to the rear of the stables."

"Thanks," Clint said.

"What if there are men waiting there, too?" Rachel asked.

"I'm sure there are, Rachel," Clint said. "Do you want to run or fight?"

"We can't run!" she said. "Everything I own is either on that buckboard or upstairs in my room."

"Let's go, then," he said, drawing his gun. "Stay behind me, and have your gun handy."

"Clint."

"Yeah?"

"I paid you," she said. "You're not responsible for me any-more, remember?"

He turned and looked at her and said, "Habit."

SIXTY-SIX

Clint and Rachel came out the kitchen door and found themselves behind the hotel. They turned right, as the cook had told them, and ran to the back of the stable. Rachel started to run to the door, but Clint grabbed her.

"Wait," he said. "There may be some men in there who aren't looking for us. We can't just shoot first and ask questions later."

"So what do we do?"

"You shoot if I do, understood?"

"Yes."

"Are you scared?"

"Yes."

"Good. Let's go."

They walked to the rear door and entered. Once inside, Clint saw two men standing by the buckboard. What he didn't know at that moment was that they'd been told by Dutch to find the buckboard and stay with it. But when Clint saw two armed men standing there, he knew what they were for. He was also pleased there were only two of them.

"'Scuse us," Clint called out.

Both men turned and looked at him.

"That's our buckboard. Can we help you?"

The two men looked at each other, then back at Clint and the gun that was already in his hand. Although Dutch and

Floyd Crater now knew who he was, none of the other men did.

"Your name Rachel?" one of the man asked.

"That's right."

They looked at each other, and Clint knew they were going for their guns.

"Don't—" he said, but it was too late.

One man simply dropped and drew, while the other threw himself behind the buckboard. Clint fired at the first man and drilled him square in the chest. The man pulled the trigger of his own gun once, and died. He was already dead when Rachel's bullet hit him.

"Shit," Clint said. "We've got to get to that buckboard."

The second man peered out from behind it and fired. Clint pushed Rachel one way and went the other. They both found cover behind hay bales.

"Rachel," he called.

"Yes?"

"You all right?"

"Yes, I'm fine."

"You've got to watch the door," he said. "Anybody shows up, keep 'em pinned down."

"What happens when I run out of bullets?"

"Hopefully," Clint said, "by then we'll have those guns in your coffin."

"Okay."

"I'm going for it now."

Clint thought he could make a run for it, as long as the buckboard was between him and the other man. He hoped that rushing him was the last thing the man would expect . . .

"I got a telegram from a Captain Jennings with the Oklahoma Police, Sheriff," the chief said, when he came back into his office. "Seems you're not one of his favorite people."

"And he's not one of mine," Brody said. "Look, Chief—"

"I'm not going to be able to help—"

At that moment a uniformed policeman rushed in and said, "Chief, there's a firefight down at the Congress Hotel. They're shootin' the place up!"

Brody was up and running without hearing the chief order, "Well, get some men over there!"

• • •

Clint rushed the buckboard, and as the man came over the top to fire at him, he dropped low and slid beneath it. Once underneath, he shot the man in the belly before he could recover. Clint rolled out from under the wagon and heard shots coming from the door. Without looking, he jumped into the buckboard bed and attacked the coffin.

Dutch and the others heard the shots as they were running for the stable, and Dutch knew that the two men he'd sent inside had already engaged Clint and Rachel.

As they reached the door, he suddenly put his arms out, stopping Luke, Sam and Del before they could rush in. That left Floyd alone as he entered the stable, and took a bullet in the chest.

Rachel shot the first man who came through the door. It wasn't her father or brother, and it wasn't Del. She assumed it was Cousin Floyd. The man staggered, pulled the trigger of his own gun twice, and went down.

Another family member dead by her hand.

Suddenly, it was quiet.

"Rachel!" Dutch shouted. "It's your pa!"

Clint had the coffin open and was taking a rifle out. He checked it and found that it was loaded. There were a couple of other rifles in there, as well as some handguns. In addition, he saw some expensive-looking silver candle holders and teapots and other household items. If there'd been any money in there—as he had long suspected—Rachel had taken it out already. If there wasn't any money, then he'd risked his life to get some guns and housewares to Austin. That prospect did not make him too happy, and he wasn't even sure he really wanted to know. The coffin and its contents could remain Rachel's business.

He beckoned for Rachel to run to him. She hesitated, but then took off running. When she reached the buckboard, he handed her a rifle.

"Get behind the coffin," he said, "and then answer him."

"Come on, Rachel," Dutch yelled, again. "It's your ol' pa. What are ya doin', girl?"

Clint grabbed another rifle from the coffin, checked to see if it was loaded, then dropped down and got behind the buckboard.

"Go 'way, Pa," Rachel shouted.

"I can't, girl," Dutch said. "Two of your brothers is dead. I can't walk away from that. And I can't walk away from all that money you took."

"It's mine, Pa."

"It was your husband's, and now that he's dead it belongs to the family."

"No, it don't," she said stubbornly. "It's mine."

"You're a foolish girl," he said. Then: "Adams, you in there?"

"I'm here!"

"This here's family business," Dutch said. "You can walk away."

"I killed more of your family than Rachel did, Crater," Clint said. "You aren't about to let me walk away."

"Die, then!" Dutch said.

"Come on, old man," Clint said. "Come and get it."

At that moment the two men Dutch had left out front came running in from the front door. They saw Clint and fired.

Dutch heard the shots and figured the other men had joined the fray.

"Okay, boys," he said. "We're goin' in. Me and Luke'll go right, Del and Sam, you go left."

"Got it!" Del said.

"Now!"

Clint turned as the two men opened fire at him, and felt something hot go into his hip. He lowered the rifle and began firing, then heard Rachel fire from above him. Both men spun and fell. As Clint and Rachel both turned to the back door, four men came rushing in.

"No, Pa!" Rachel shouted, and started firing.

The four men sought cover as soon as they entered, but that split second of not knowing the interior of the stable cost them. Sam looked around and saw the bale of hay his sister had been hiding behind just moments before, but by the time he decided to go for it, she had shot him in the chest. He yelled, spun and fell.

Clint drew his revolver with his right hand, holding the rifle in his left, and fired twice. He didn't know who he hit, but it was Luke. Both bullets struck him, belly and chest, and he crumpled.

Dutch made it to one hay bale, Del made it to the other, and it got quiet again.

SIXTY-SEVEN

"Damn it, Rachel!" Dutch shouted. "You're pissin' me off now, gal!"

"Go away, Pa!"

"Can't do that now," Dutch said. "Adams knows that. Right, Adams?"

"Too much has happened, Dutch," Clint said. "Doesn't look like anybody's going to just walk away from this."

"You killed all my boys," Dutch said.

"You still got one left, Dutch," Clint said. "Why not save him?"

"He ain't my son," Dutch said. "My sons are dead. He ain't nothin' to me. Only child I got left is Rachel."

"You lost me a long time ago, Pa."

"I'm gonna step out, Adams," Dutch said. "It'll just be you and me. Let's get it over with."

"What about your other—the other one?"

"Del won't do nothin'," Dutch said. "Will ya, Del?"

There was some hesitation; then Del said, "No, Dutch."

"Whataya say, Adams?" Dutch called.

"Okay, Dutch," Clint said. "Let's put an end to it."

"Don't shoot me, gal," Dutch sad. "I'm comin' out."

"I won't shoot, Pa."

Dutch stood up and stepped out from cover. He had his gun in his holster, and his hands held away from his side.

Clint stepped out, and set the rifle down on the buckboard.

"Take 'im, Del!" Dutch suddenly shouted.

Clint tensed, but there was no shot.

"Del! Kill 'im."

"You told me not to do anything, Dutch," Del said. The younger man stood up and tossed his gun out. "That's what I'm doin'."

"Wha—What's wrong with you, boy?"

"Nothin'," Del said. "I just found out I ain't anythin' to you, Dutch, even after all these years. Guess you ain't anythin' to me, either." Del looked at Clint. "I'm leavin.'"

"Go," Clint said.

Del turned and walked out of the stable.

"Well, Dutch," Clint said. "You and me, like you said."

"Sonofabitch coward!" Dutch shouted.

Clint would never know if the man had been yelling at him or Del. Dutch went for his gun and Clint drew smoothly and gunned down Rachel's father right in front of her.

Dutch fell onto his back and lay still.

Rachel dropped down from the buckboard and looked at her father's body.

"I'm sorry, Rachel."

"Don't be, Clint," she said. "This was how it had to end."

They heard men running behind them and both turned, guns ready. First they saw Carl Brody, and then behind him a bunch of uniformed policemen.

"It's all over, Sheriff," Clint said.

"I missed it?" Brody asked.

"You didn't miss anything," Clint said, holstering his gun. "Not anything at all."